Washtenaw Library for the Blind and Physically Disabled @ AADL

If you are only able to read large print, you may qualify for WLBPD @ AADL services, including receiving audio and large print books by mail at no charge.

For more information:

Email   wlbpd@aadl.org
Phone   (734) 327-4224
Website   wlbpd.aadl.org

SETTLERS' HOPE

SETTLERS' HOPE

KATHLEEN D. BAILEY

THORNDIKE PRESS
A part of Gale, a Cengage Company

Thorndike Press, a part of Gale, a Cengage Company.

ALL RIGHTS RESERVED
Thorndike Press® Large Print Christian Romance.
The text of this Large Print edition is unabridged.
Other aspects of the book may vary from the original edition.
Set in 16 pt. Plantin.

LIBRARY OF CONGRESS CIP DATA ON FILE.
CATALOGUING IN PUBLICATION FOR THIS BOOK
IS AVAILABLE FROM THE LIBRARY OF CONGRESS.

ISBN-13: 979-8-8857-8243-2 (hardcover alk. paper)

Published in 2022 by arrangement with White Rose Publishing, a
division of Pelican Ventures, LLC.

Printed in Mexico
Print Number : 1   Print Year : 2023

To my husband David W. Bailey,
who has never let go of helping me
achieve my dreams.

1

January 1847
Hall's Mill, The Oregon Country

In his career, Pace Williams had confronted Mexican bandits, wagon train mutinies, white men's pistols, red men's tomahawks, and a man in the Canadian lumber camp who had gone berserk and charged the entire company with an axe. But he'd never been pushed into a water trough by a woman with a perfect face and eyes the color of a mountain stream.

He struggled to his feet, shaking himself like a dog. The water was cold enough. At least it wasn't raining, the rain that dripped or pounded its way through every day of an Oregon Country winter.

This woman knew how to get a man's attention; he'd give her that although there must be easier ways.

His best friend, Michael Moriarty, clambered out of the trough, with his wife, Caroline, clinging to him as though she could lift two hundred pounds of muscled Irishman. Mike looked as sorry as Pace felt, with his denims and plaid shirt sticking to him. Their friends' and neighbors' laughter didn't help any.

Mike leveled a glare at them before focusing it on the newcomer.

"Moriarty, who is she?" someone from the crowd called out.

"She's Oona Cathleen Moriarty, my sister. And she's supposed to be in a convent in Dublin, not pushing me into horses' troughs."

The woman matched him, scowl for scowl. "After what you did to me, 'tis a blessing I didn't drown you. Putting me in a convent? Could not even you have thought of something better?" Her voice was melodious with Mike's Irish lilt, sweeter than her words or her expression.

She looked like a scarecrow in a wool coat with a button missing, stall-mucking boots, and a man's shapeless felt hat. But the face under the hat was the best one Pace had seen in a while. An oval face, with full red lips, skin like fresh cream, and big eyes with long dark lashes.

And angry. Very angry.

Mike crossed his soggy arms. "How did

you get here?"

"Steerage ship, wagon train, freighter." Oona Moriarty ticked them off on her fingers. "And a few interesting conveyances in between. I hitched one ride with a man who was driving a hearse. An empty one — he was delivering it to a funeral parlor," she clarified.

She was playing the crowd, and they loved it. Whatever she'd been, whatever she'd become, she was still a Moriarty, this performance marking her more than the blue eyes and black hair. Mike always loved an audience, even in the darkest of times.

Mike shivered as he stared at her.

"Maybe we should get you into some dry clothes," Caroline murmured, her gaze locked on this unexpected sister-in-law as if Oona would burst into flames.

But their friend, Jenny Thatcher, took charge. "Michael, go home, get into some dry duds. I'll take your sister back to the hotel and find her something to eat." Jenny always knew what was best for everyone and wasn't shy about showing it.

The townspeople continued to point, to chuckle. It'd be nice if they all went home, but Pace knew his neighbors. That was too much to ask.

Every person who could walk or be carried was in the village today to watch the freighters from the east roll in. They were wagons like the "prairie schooners" that had brought most of Hall's Mill west, but larger and without the canvas roofs. These wagons bulged with crates, barrels, and indefinable shapes, all lashed together with stout ropes. Teams of oxen pulled the wagons, and huge, weary-looking men trudged beside them, goads at the ready. Teamsterin'. One of the few legal things Pace hadn't done.

Pace's glance passed over a pigtailed Chinese man, a smattering of Injuns. The settlement's only black family stood a little apart as they always did.

The faces differed in color, but had one thing in common. None of them was old. Any elderly had been weeded out on the sixth-month overland journey or had sense enough not to come in the first place. The West was young people's country.

It wasn't raining. But the air was still damp, mixed with the odor of smoke struggling from the poorly ventilated shacks and the heady smell of new-cut lumber from the mill. And the mud churned up by the teamsters' wheels.

A shiver ran through Pace.

A logger from one of the camps slapped

him on the back. "You all right, Mr. Williams?"

"Yeah, Owens. Thanks."

People liked him here. Might be a good place to put down roots, if only he'd had roots. If anyone had the skills to wrest a living from these green forests, this rich land, Pace did. He had farmed, ranched, logged, and worked on the docks of a seaport city. And he'd led wagonloads of starry-eyed fools from the States to here. Make a living in the Oregon Territory? Child's play.

Would it be today? Would these wagons bring direction for the next step of his journey? Did he want them to? Pace was thirty. He'd been on the run for nineteen years. Maybe the trip would end here, at the edge of the known world. He was tired of running, tired of checking every wagon train for their faces. The prison term was up this year. Yeah, he'd kept count. What would they look like now? Old. Mean. The meanness that had been as much a part of them as breathing. The kind of meanness a body didn't outgrow, didn't have beaten out of them.

Nobody came to Hall's Mill without a reason. Few people even knew it existed. They'd never track him here. Would they?

Well, he couldn't stand around all day. He

had a run to make. But first, he had to find some dry clothes. And second — he mentally rubbed his hands together — he had words to have with Mike's sister.

Oona allowed the one called Jenny to shepherd her toward a single-story building that Jenny assured her was a hotel. The building looked like the doll houses she and her sister Orla used to make out of packing crates. She'd take Jenny's word for it. Nothing in Hall's Mill looked built to last, but it didn't matter. She wouldn't be here long enough to find out.

Could she pull it off? This trip had taken everything Oona had, financially, emotionally, physically.

And Michael was married. Well, that was a complication, but nothing she couldn't handle. She'd spent three, no, four years planning for this, and a lifetime before that sharpening her wits against five brothers and three sisters. She could manage Michael.

How could Michael live in a place like this? Worse than she'd expected, worse than the other pilgrims had told her, with its one street of mud and the ramshackle buildings, with the rain that broke for maybe an hour a day. Was this why the people on the wagon trains sold their farms and businesses, said good-bye to loved ones forever? *This* was their Promised Land?

Some parts of it could be tolerable. She peered over her shoulder, hoping to catch a glimpse of the tall man she'd dunked along with Michael. Teach *him* to laugh at her.

He was good-looking enough, but she had no intention of getting mixed up with some cowboy. Not with the job she had to do. Get what she came for, that's what she'd do, and leave this raw and dirty place behind. Shake off the dust from her feet.

Or the mud.

2

Pace edged closer to the open hearth. Except for his feet he was dry, thanks to a dash home to change into clean pants and shirt. Wasn't nothing he could do about his feet. The only dry socks he had were several days past clean. Just one more thing to blame on the beautiful, babbling stranger.

Caroline and a dry-clad Mike flanked Miss Moriarty at the kitchen table of the modest Hall's Mill Inn. Behind them, Jenny kneaded the next day's bread, and the first drops of a new rainstorm spattered the windows. Dishes clattered as Sadie, the mute kitchen girl, washed them in the background. There was never any telling what Sadie understood or didn't, but Pace didn't care. The whole world could hear Oona Moriarty's explanation, just as long as he did. He gave her his best scowl, the one that had subdued many a stubborn pilgrim to the West.

But she went on chatting with Mike between bites of fresh bread, spoonsful of stew, and sips of tea. As if she hadn't done anything.

Maybe he could get some dry socks from Mike. Mike had stuff like that. Pace didn't. He did his own laundry, rinsing clothes out in a creek when they got stiff. Maybe he could ask Mike, or Caroline. That is, if the sister ever stopped talking.

"Of course I wasn't staying," Oona said in answer to Mike's question about the convent. " 'Twas never my plan. I just wanted to be safe until you got out of the country. I thought the whole business with Mr. Hawthorne would die down."

It hadn't — anything but. The Moriartys' English landlord had not forgotten his son's death. This wasn't the place or time to tell her, though. Not with Caroline still staring at this new relative as if Oona was about to explode.

It was almost funny. Mike near speechless from the shock of seeing his sister. Mike without words.

Mike managed, just barely, to croak out another question. "When did you leave?"

Oona talked around a crust of bread. How long since she'd eaten?

"The convent? Nigh on to a year ago. I

15

managed fairly well during the postulant and novice stages. Except for the obedience and keeping silence parts," she added, a frown marring her smooth brow. "But it was coming on to my third year, and we're supposed to take our first vows. Michael, I couldn't vow something I didn't believe was for me. So I left. They gave me a lecture, five pounds. I got a job as a maid and saved up my passage, and then I was a governess in New York and worked until I had money for the wagon train."

Pace shifted his wet feet and moved closer to the fire. The water sloshed in his boots, so loud one could hear it.

Jenny quirked an eyebrow at him.

He'd hear about this. It wasn't his fault. This Oona Moriarty, now, she was out of line. Weren't *her* feet rotting inside *her* boots.

He was cold and already tired, and he had a delivery to make. Funny how cold feet could make the rest of your body feel like an icicle. He'd been through worse than this, much worse, bringing cattle in from the high pasture during a fall storm, falling into a creek in the logging camp. Hiding in wet clothes from men who meant him no good. Didn't make this time any easier. *Getting soft, Pace.*

16

"I came over in the steerage," Oona was saying. "And I can tell you, it made the wagon train look easy."

Nothing made a wagon train look easy. No woman made light of the westward journey, and few undertook it alone. Brave as well as pretty, this one.

But Pace had a delivery to make, he couldn't stand around jawin' all day. "Miss Moriarty."

She swiveled to face him, those blue eyes so like Mike's and deceptively full of innocence.

"Why'd you dunk *me*? I never did anything to you."

The girl didn't miss a beat. "Because you were there. And you were laughing."

So was the rest of the town.

"Thank you to keep your hands to yourself in the future."

She sized him up with a slow grin he didn't much like. "I will do that, Mr. — Mr. —"

"This is Pace Williams, the trail boss. I worked for him," Mike inserted.

Oona Moriarty dimpled, and held out the hand that wasn't feeding her. " 'Tis pleased I am to make your acquaintance, Mr. Pace Williams."

He shook her hand briefly. Long slender

fingers, soft skin — when had he touched anything that good? "Pleased to meet you, too." He wasn't really, but she'd probably figured that out.

Oona. The sister who had killed the landlord's son, smashing a stone on his head to keep him from harming Mike.

He dropped her hand as though scalded. Shaking hands with a murderess. Self-defense, but still . . .

"I got to go, got to make a delivery up the mountain." He turned to leave, he hoped with dignity, but his wet socks squeaked in his boots.

Oona looked after Pace Williams. Interesting man, tall, with that deep tan and crinkles around his eyes, the dark brown eyes that had held hers too briefly in the square. Was he taken? Probably. Anyway, that wasn't what she was here for.

Michael interrupted her thoughts. "The others. What happened to them? I got just the one letter from Uncle Eamon, tellin' me Ma was dead."

She heard the plea in his voice, the loss even his Caroline couldn't fill. Oh, these three years had been just as hard on him.

"Well, Ma died on the trip. You know that. After — after they got evicted from the cot-

18

tage." Dead in a ditch from starvation on the long walk to Uncle Eamon, the only relative who had room for an evicted family.

"What about the others? What about Tom?"

"I do not know. When I got out, I asked about him. Eamon hasn't heard from him."

Michael put his head in his hands, as she'd known he would. He would not ask about the "littles," the three youngest Moriartys. If she couldn't find Tom, their oldest brother, she wouldn't find the children.

Caroline stroked his arm, and leaned her head against his shoulder. She was a pretty little thing, with heart-shaped face, big hazel eyes, and light brown hair escaping from her bun to curl around her face. Not what Michael's type had been, but anyone could change. And in the old days, almost everyone had been Michael's type.

He lifted his face to look at Oona again. "So why did you come?"

Better a half-answer. She was good at those. "You're all I have left. I was afraid to stay in Ireland. Afraid of Hawthorne's men, afraid they'd find me. That they'd figure it out."

"Well." Michael cleared his throat. "That's not happenin' soon. Two of 'em tracked me across the country. They caught up with us in the Blue Mountains, and now they're dead."

"There will be others." There were always others.

"But they'll never find us here. This is as far West as we can get. And *nobody* comes to Hall's Mill."

Oona couldn't argue that. She already wished she hadn't. But she knew he would.

"What about Kevin? Did you try to find *him*?"

Kevin O'Halloran. The genial young man who'd asked for Oona's hand before all their worlds suffered a sea-change. Oona took a deep breath. When would it stop hurting? "Kevin's dead, Michael. He was in the underground, going to meetings, and he got on the wrong side of some landlord. Not Hawthorne, but just as mean. The members of his cell found him strung from a tree."

"I did not know Kevin was political."

"I did." Oona was silent for a minute, going back to a time when they were all young and Ireland offered as much hope as it ever would.

The English, their overlords. Would they never stop taking? She was years removed from the village. She'd thought they couldn't hurt her here.

"Well," Michael said. "You can't stay."

She put down her spoon. "And why not?"

" 'Tis obvious. We don't have the room." He looked to his wife for help, but she just stared back, with a spine Oona wouldn't have expected. This was Michael's fight.

Jenny, the pretty blonde, turned from the stove. "You can stay in my room. I got two beds. I just need to find a pillow and blankets. And Molly, she's the one who owns this place, she might have some work for you."

Michael gave Jenny a dirty look before he transferred it to Oona. There was plenty to go around. "But it isn't — you can't —"

She could argue him into a hole. "It's a free country. Isn't that why you're here?"

"There's nothing here for you. Not for a single woman, and one not used to our ways."

Our ways. Yes, he was an American now. "I'll pick them up. I'm not leaving, Michael." Not yet, anyway. Not 'til she'd gotten what she came for from him.

"It's not safe here."

"It's as safe as it is for your wife." She jerked her head toward Caroline. That one. She'd probably scream if she saw a mouse. Alive or dead.

"But she has a husband."

"But I have my wits. And a brother."

Michael shrugged. "Well, then. We'll see. You've got a place for tonight."

Michael stood and stretched, his hands almost touching the ceiling. For him, it was over. Nice to be Michael. He'd always been like this, able to move on.

"Oona, why here? Why did you not go to Ohio, to Uncle James?"

Why, indeed? She'd have to tell him, but not tonight. Not with Caroline and Jenny, and the mute girl for all she knew, hanging on every word. Get him used to her again, get *her* used to this new Michael and his wife. Get her sea legs — or in this case, her land legs. A lot of land, and unlike anything she'd seen before.

A man like that Pace, now, he belonged here. As if he'd been carved from one of the soaring pines she'd seen on the way in. But there was a guarded look in his eyes . . . and was she the only one who sensed a kind of sorrow? Oona knew about sorrow.

She was physically tired after walking and riding across a continent. And she was tired of smiling, joking, being brave because there was no other way to be. Was Pace like her, had he played a role for so long he'd forgotten who he was?

Well, she wouldn't find out today.

And in the meantime, she'd bluff. She was

good at that. She'd learned it from Michael. She gave him her most brilliant smile. "Uncle James never liked me any more than he liked you. Michael, take me home with you and show me where Caroline keeps her foodstuffs. I'll rest a bit and then I'll make us all a good supper, so I will. A celebration supper. And then I'll move in with Jenny."

3

Pace made two crisp knocks on the splintered door of the Moriartys' cabin. Though the rain fell in sheets around him, his turned-up collar kept most of it off. Too bad he couldn't have done something about his feet, even wetter now after a ride up the mountain and back. He knocked once more, just to be sure, then lifted the rusted iron latch, and stared down the barrel of a shotgun, with a pair of thick-lashed blue eyes boring into his.

Oona Moriarty with a weapon.

Just what he needed.

Pace splayed back against the door and stuck his hands in the air. He gulped out a, "Whoa. Ma'am, you want to put that thing away?"

"Oh, 'tis you again. What is your business with my brother?"

"I'm his best friend," Pace growled. "His only friend, come to that. I had to change my clothes after you so kindly dunked me, and I stopped by the livery stable on the way back to see if he had any clean, dry socks. He said I could borrow a pair. That good enough?"

Oona Moriarty backed up a little. The gun lowered a fraction. "Why don't *you* have clean dry socks?"

Best not to follow his first instinct, which was to grab the gun from her. "Because he has a wife and I don't."

The woman carefully placed the shotgun on the table, a barrel topped with a board. "Well then, Mr. Williams. Would you be wantin' a cup of tea?"

It sounded good — his entire body was damp now, not just his feet. "Can I have the socks, too?"

Mike's sister waved toward the wooden crates that held the couple's clothing.

Pace snagged a towel, too, and rubbed his reddened feet. As he pulled on the dry socks he ventured, "Miss, you know how to fire that thing?"

"We would have found out, wouldn't we?" the woman said with her back to him.

There was no good answer to that.

Like Pace's, the Moriartys' shack had a small fireplace with no chimney, just a vent direct to the outside. The woman bent, deftly removed an iron pot from its hook, and poured water into two tin cups.

Well, she knew her way around a kitchen, even this pathetic excuse for one.

" 'Tis not like any tea I've ever tasted, and there's no milk or sugar, but 'tis hot."

Perched on another barrel, he cradled the mug in his chilled hands. "The Injun women make it from a plant. It ain't bad. Better'n what passes for coffee around here."

The woman flipped her black braid behind her as she settled on a stool with a log for its third leg. "When I came in on the freighters, I saw sacks of coffee and crates of tea. At one point, I sat on a crate of pure, East India tea. There'll be decent tea by nightfall."

A gunshot ripped through the air, and the woman flinched.

Pace put out a hand to steady her.

She froze for a second, looking up at him as his touch lingered on her arm.

He pulled away quickly. What was *that* all about? "It's all right, ma'am," he said when he'd found his voice. "Some boys got a hold of some firecrackers. They was on the freighters. I don't know who ordered them, but they ain't harmful. Only loud."

Oona relaxed. "Faith, and don't I know about little boys. I had five brothers."

Pace found her use of the word faith endearing. He'd heard Michael say the same thing from time to time and it had taken him a bit to learn it was an expression the Irish sometimes used.

They sipped the bitter but warming brew, in makeshift chairs on either side of a makeshift table in this makeshift house. By Hall's Mill standards, the Moriarty place wasn't bad. Rain pelted the plank door. But the roof wasn't leaking — yet.

Over the rim of his cup, Pace studied Oona Moriarty. As tall as Jenny but curvier, with that thick braid of black hair swinging almost to her waist. Her blue eyes were like Mike's, in a perfect oval face. Her firm jaw, hinting at stubbornness, was Michael's in feminine form. Pace wondered what that hair would look like loose. She was — she was beautiful, no other word for it. Were there any others like her back in Ireland?

From what he'd heard, this one was probably enough.

"You're the one killed the landlord's son." He placed his tin cup on the table like a gauntlet.

" 'Tis me." The dark blue eyes never wavered; the voice never broke. "Michael let everyone think it was him. I guess you know that by now."

"You're the one who was a nun."

"I was a novice, not a nun. Michael and Tom — my oldest brother — they put me in a convent for safekeeping after I killed young Mr. Hawthorne. I stayed a while. Then I left and went looking for my family."

And dunked Pace in a water trough, pulled a gun on him, then served him herbal tea.

It explained a lot.

"What do *you* do, Mr. Williams?"

He swallowed, let the warmth course through him, and then answered. "Here, I'm a courier. I run stuff out to the homesteads and the camps. But I'm a wagon master by trade. This year I decided to winter over. Mike and Caroline and our friend Jenny are fixin' on staying. They got good jobs, Mike at the livery stable, Caroline at the store, Jenny at the hotel. We was lucky."

Lucky to be alive, lucky to be together. How much had Mike told her? Did she know about the cholera, the wagon train mutiny, the shootout in the Blue Mountains?

She'd find out soon enough.

Was that a scream?

Pace bolted from the cabin with the Mo-

28

riarty woman on his heels.

A wagon careened through Hall's Mill's excuse for a town square. A frightened farm wife pulled on the reins of two horses that had no intention of stopping. Three big-eyed children huddled in the back. The horses' eyes were rolled back so the whites showed, and their neighing sent a chill through even him.

The danged firecrackers. Kids had nothing better to do. Kids had no business —

Pace jumped on a mounting block and flung himself onto the seat beside the woman. He grabbed the reins, but these two nags had minds of their own. He tossed the reins back to the woman, poised himself at the front of the wagon, bent his knees, and took a flying leap.

He bit his lip until he tasted blood. He knew better than to look down. Jumping on the back of the gray gelding, he pulled on the bit with his bare hands. The gray turned to look at him, almost in disbelief, before it dug its front hooves into the mud. The bay continued to lurch forward. Pace managed the gray with his left hand and catapulted onto the back of the bay. He grabbed the bit. The bay strained and reared up, and Pace dug his thighs into its flanks. Well, there were worse ways to die. He finally dared to look back. "Ma'am, you all right?"

"Thank you, sir. Oh, thank you," the woman babbled. She had the played-out look of someone who hadn't wanted to come here in the first place. Like most of the women. The West was a man's dream.

The kids now felt free to cry, and the woman gathered the smallest one into her lap.

"Wasn't nothing, ma'am. Be careful with this horse in town. Some boys got a hold of some firecrackers yesterday. They even spooked me."

No time to think. That was the way he liked things.

Oona Moriarty held the door for him. Her face was ashen, but even now, she had something to say. "I have never seen anything like that in my entire life."

Pace shrugged and picked up his still-hot tea. "Your brother can do it faster. I clocked him one time at three minutes."

Wasn't nothing, really. He'd done this before. Done most anything that required good nerves, maybe a gun, and not much thought.

Praise made him nervous, always had, so he shifted the talk to her. "How do you find America?"

Oona Moriarty's smile transformed her

face. Not that it needed transforming. "Mr. Williams, it's better than all the stories and then some. I was a governess in New York, and every day I saw something new, something big, something special. Then I went on the wagon train, and I saw even more. It's like — it's like ten countries rolled into one."

"Trail wasn't too rough?"

Oona shrugged. "I had only myself to think of. I shared a wagon with an older couple. They were in their forties, and I helped them with the work, but we weren't family. At Fort Hall, they split off for California, and I came the rest of the way by freighter."

She was pretty. The loose dress in a muddy brown could not disguise her shape. The firelight played off her shiny black hair and made her face glow. She was the best thing he had seen in a while. He had to admit it.

Oona poured more hot water over the soggy herbs. "I'm sure I'll find work. Jenny said she'd get me on at the hotel. She's really nice."

Jenny Thatcher was all right. Jenny had saved *his* hide more than once.

"And I really like Caroline," Oona babbled on. A Moriarty to the core. "She's so sweet

31

and perfect for Michael."

Caroline *was* sweet, and smart, and tough, and easy on the eyes. Caroline was a lot of things, including the reason Mike left the trail, staying on in Hall's Mill to homestead.

And this was the first time Pace had been lonely. Was it seeing Mike with Caroline, the completeness that radiated from them?

Until Caroline O'Leary landed back in his life, Mike had been as rootless as Pace.

Was Pace tired of running? They'd never think to look for him here. Would anyone ever *want* him to stay? This Oona. He couldn't take his eyes off her. What would it be like to come home to her, to *make* a home with her? "Mike has changed," he said after a pause. "Caroline tell you he got religion?"

"Um, no." She set her cup down. *"Michael?"*

"He and Caroline are running Bible studies in the hotel dining room every Sunday." He had the satisfaction of seeing her jaw drop, just a little.

"Bible studies. Michael." She chewed on that for a full minute. "Do you go?"

He'd done fine without God all these years, and maybe a little better than he would have. Hadn't thought much about God since 1828 when God had been absent

32

on the worst night of his life. "Miss Moriarty, I am not a Bible kind of guy." He stood up and put his tin cup on the table. "I got to go. Thanks for the socks and the tea."

"Thank Michael. They're his socks."

She got up too, and in the crowded room, she stood closer than she needed to. Closer than he'd hoped. He could smell her hair and skin, like that stuff "she" used to use in baking. Vanilla?

"You could stay," Oona said. "I've made supper for Michael and Caroline." She gestured toward the hearth, where something simmered that smelled wonderful in an entirely different way.

"No. I got to go." For more reasons than one. "See, Jenny brings me supper from the hotel every night."

"Oh."

So it's like that, her tone conveyed the true meaning of the word. It wasn't. But if he stayed here much longer whatever "it" was wouldn't have a chance, and Mike's sister was dangerous. Life was dangerous enough without getting mixed up with a murderer, a novice, and a Moriarty.

Oona thought about Pace Williams as she made up her new bed in Jenny's room. A fine-looking man, tall, and confident in his movements. If western men were all like this, faith, and it might be fun here. Truth be told, before the ocean crossing and New York, she hadn't seen any man but her priest for three full years. First thing she'd had to get used to was the voices. This Pace had a nice deep voice. Might be interesting to get to know him. And wasn't he the brave one, jumping on that runaway horse? A man like this Pace could do anything, be anything.

She'd noticed him this morning in the square, even before the dunking. Their gazes had connected, and she'd had to force herself to look away. Did he remember? Had his world shifted on its axis? Had he felt as though he'd known her all his life? Had he felt what she felt when she handed him the tin cup and their fingers touched? When the first firecracker went off and he'd steadied her?

Impossible.

She just wasn't used to being around men. Let a nice one come around, and her imagination went wild. Anyway, she wasn't here for that. And if he knew her real purpose for coming West . . . She had a job to do, and she was the only one who could do it.

Tonight, she'd made supper for Michael and Caroline and endured more of his objections to her being there. The chief one seemed to be her safety, and she had to laugh. Where had he been when she'd crossed the ocean in steerage, holding the heads of fellow passengers as they puked, and sometimes died? Where had he been in New York, when she'd constantly evaded the grasping hands of her employer's associates? Where had he been when she'd taken off to the West to find him? Was she afraid? Yes. Would she ever let him know it? Never.

No time to think. Now she had the time and she shivered, drawing the one rough blanket around her shoulders.

She had killed a man. She'd escaped her punishment, hiding in the convent, crossing an ocean, a desert, and a chain of mountains. Her family was splintered, if they were still alive. Because of her.

Her oldest brother, Tom, who hadn't asked for any of this, who only wanted to farm, to someday raise his own family, to attend Mass and market day in the time-worn tradition of their people. Tom, who had helped Michael rescue her against any of their better judgments. She could still see Tom's reproachful face as he hauled her off to the convent in Dublin.

Orla, the oldest sister, but more like a twin to Oona. Nine months between them. They did chores in tandem, shared clothes, flirted with the village lads, step-danced at the *ceili* parties. Well, Orla had married off the estate so she was already gone, but now she'd disappeared into the mist with the rest of them.

Caitrin, their only redhead. Fiercely religious, heartbreakingly beautiful, a tough tomboy. If anyone could handle what Ireland could throw at a person, it would be Caitrin. But they would never know. She'd disappeared somewhere along the trail to Uncle Eamon's.

The littles, the ones Oona had helped raise as an older sister. No, she wouldn't think about the littles.

Oona hadn't led the Hawthorne boy on. She was promised to Kevin, and she'd liked it that way. But Hawthorne had sought her out, and tried to take what he wanted. And she had reacted, not to save herself, but to save Michael. But dead was still dead.

The blood pooled on the flagstone floor of Squire Hawthorne's barn. Young Hawthorne's lifeless eyes in a masklike face had stared.

She'd chanted her prayers along with the other sisters in the dim Abbey chapel, as hundreds of votive lights flickered. She'd made confessions to her priest and in the weekly chapter meetings. But she'd never confessed this. Where to begin? Could God forgive a murderess? No. There was only one way to make it right, and that was without God.

And *Michael* had religion now.

She breathed a laugh. Well, good luck to him. If he wanted, he could have her share too.

4

"Pace, hey Pace, you in there?"

Pace roused himself at the familiar voice, the light knock. "Come in. You know it's open." Usually was. Nobody in Hall's Mill had anything worth stealing.

Jenny pushed her way inside. She carried a tray with two steaming covered bowls, a platter of sliced bread, and —

Oh, let it be slabs of pie.

"Beef stew, fresh bread, and what's left of the blueberry pie," she announced. "That's it 'til summer unless the freighters brought in some canned fruit."

"Lookin' good," Pace said. But then, so did Jenny.

She placed the food on an overturned barrel, his table, and lowered herself gracefully to the other end of his pallet. She sat tailor-style, tucking her long legs under her skirt. Her blonde hair was tamed in a short braid, and shining in the firelight.

"You make this?"

"The bread an' the pie," she said around a mouthful.

They dined together almost every night. They were both alone, Jenny had pointed out soon after she got the hotel job. And she got her meals free; weren't no trouble to put together a plate of leftovers for Pace. Saved him having to cook, the one thing he'd never learned to do. And Jenny was good company, even if only for an hour.

"Pass is open," she said. "You could leave."

Pace savored a mouthful of stew. Yes, he could go. Iffen he wanted to. "No hurry. St. Joe will be there when I get back, 'long with a passel of fools wanting to go west."

Jenny snorted. "Ain't that the truth. Remember the ones who left us at Fort Hall? Wonder if they made it to Californy."

"I don't wonder." Because he didn't care.

Pace sprawled on his pallet, a mug of reheated coffee in his hands and his stock-inged feet stuck out in front of him. Rain pattered against the roof of his cabin, a not so bad feeling if one was indoors with a fire and coffee. He'd seen enough times when he wasn't. Rain pinged, a drop at a time, into a tin saucepan at one of the roof joints. He supposed he should fix it, but he wasn't planning on staying long enough for it to

39

matter. And if he did stay, it wouldn't be in this dump.

Jenny had all the town gossip from the hotel and restaurant. Didn't talk much about herself, but she was a good listener. She picked up on things. Should he ask her about Mike's sister, that strange and beautiful lady who had come out of nowhere? Something held him back. He waited, concentrating on his food. He wouldn't go first.

"Mike's sister is a caution. Seen her push him and you," Jenny said.

Pace let out the breath he hadn't realized he was holding. "Yeah. She pulled a gun on me, too."

Jenny's eyes were as round as her pies. "Really?"

"I was going by his place to borrow some socks, and she thought I was a thief. So she's bunkin' with you?" He already knew the answer.

"Yeah. And Molly's gonna give her a few hours' work a week. It'll be nice for Mike to have some family around."

"She stayin'?"

"Dunno. Looks like she don't have much to go back to."

Neither did Pace.

He wanted to hear more, to gather every

40

scrap of information he could, to make sense of this Oona person. But Jenny had moved on, to a funny story about a gang of boys and somebody's chickens. Though Pace tried to follow, his mind wandered. Did that a lot these days.

Jenny moseyed on into a story about a saloon fight, one she hadn't seen but that was the talk of what passed for a town here.

Pace let the words ripple over him as he did every evening. He watched her, the slanted blue eyes and the high cheekbones, the fair hair like a crown, growing out since she'd cropped it to pass as a man. They had known each other for years, from her days of entertaining men in St. Joseph to her stint as one of his wagon train scouts to now. Who knew they'd find themselves in Oregon Country, she working as a waitress/cook, he hauling goods to outlying farms and lumber camps, eating dinner together in a leaky cabin on the edge of the known world. But then he'd never imagined himself doing most of the other things he'd done. In Pace's world, one didn't think ahead. One did the next thing.

What did people think about Jenny and him? She came over every night but never stayed more than an hour. She had a reputation to protect for the first time since she was fourteen. Of course, some people saw them as a couple just because they spent more time with each other than with anyone else. Could they *be* a couple?

She had come to him once on the overland journey, more from boredom and irritation than anything else, and he had sent her away. He didn't fool around with women on the trail. Wasn't professional. But now? Could they pick up where they'd left off in St. Joe? He'd be careful. Nobody needed to know. And they had been good together. And she must be as lonely as he was.

But they were friends now, and that made all the difference. As he looked at Jenny yammering away in the firelight, he knew he couldn't have done it even if she'd wanted to. Too much had passed between them. He respected her now, dang it. If he had needs, better to go down to the cribs — the shacks even worse than these — where dull-eyed women entertained loggers in town on a break. It would cost him, but Jenny would cost him more.

Or could he make an honest woman of her, strike out in this new land with her at his side? They'd been through enough together. Nobody knew him as well as Jenny did, at least to the point he wanted to be known.

Usually, by now, he'd be back east, holed up in a room somewhere, St. Joe or Independence, corresponding with people to set up next year's wagon train. This year he'd stayed on until well after the pass was closed. It was open again, some kind of January thaw, but he'd wait a few more weeks. He had a job and a roof over his head, sort of. Wasn't no need to hurry.

And Oona was here. Well, he had to stay around and see how that turned out. Didn't he?

He and Jenny had been through so much together. Bad times and good. " 'Member the buffalo hunt?"

"That was a good day."

They wouldn't talk of the darker things they'd faced, things that knit them together with invisible cords.

Jenny scraped her plate into a bucket and looked over at his. As usual, there was nothing to scrape. She stretched gracefully in the firelight. "We ridin' Sunday?"

"Don't see why not."

Jenny slanted a grin his way. "No Bible study? Caroline keeps askin'."

"I'm a godless heathen, Jen. You know that."

God had given them a wide berth. So far, he and Jenny, and a day cantering through wooded paths was as good a way as any to spend Sunday. Good enough for now, and now was where Pace Williams lived.

5

Oona watched as Jenny brushed out her hair. It fell just below her shoulders, shorter than most adult women's. There was a story there somewhere. Oona loved stories.

"Jenny, how did you come to do this? To be here?" Oona waved her night-gowned arm, a gesture that encompassed not only this tinder box of a building but the settlement on the edge of a continent in a place that wasn't even a country.

Jenny paused in her brushing then went back to it with quicker, agitated strokes. "I came here on account of Michael. Them two lowlifes from your hometown was after Mike, and I had to warn him. He would have done the same for me."

Oona stretched on her hard bed. Their work day was done, a long and demanding one but nothing she wasn't used to. They'd earned the right to relax, to chat a bit. She'd been a staff member at the house in New

York, somewhere between a maid and a family member, so she hadn't talked much to adults. And conversation at the convent had been discouraged. Maybe she and this Jenny would be friends. "Why did you cut your hair?"

"I had to dress like a man on the trail. Worked for a while."

Well, Oona couldn't see it. Jenny was as female as she was, slender but not that slender. Maybe people on the trail had other things on their minds. But Jenny was beautiful, with that spun-gold hair, big, cornflower blue eyes, and clear skin. She couldn't have fooled too many people for too long.

"How did you know my brother?"

Jenny placed the brush on the scarred bureau they shared. "How do you think I did?"

It couldn't be. Not even Michael —

"You were a — a loose woman?"

"Loose enough. I was a saloon girl in St. Joseph. Mike was my customer. Pace, too, come to think of it." Jenny climbed up on her own bed and hugged her knees to her chest. "I never went upstairs, but I used my looks to make men spend money. And I was good at it."

But saloons? Saloon girls? If it had even been a choice.

46

Whatever friendship they would have depended on Oona's next words. "It's all right," she said after a pause. "I was a novice, about to become a nun. And I didn't like it any better."

Jenny began to grin, the quick ear-to-ear grin Oona had glimpsed before. "Really?" She swore softly, stringing words together in a sequence Oona had never heard before. "Well. Ain't we the pair."

Oona agreed silently.

"Have you worked here long?" she asked.

"Since we landed here in November. We was lucky. We all got jobs — Mike at the livery, Caroline at the store, Pace deliverin' stuff."

"Is Mrs. Davis easy to work for?"

"Molly works us hard, but she's fair. She started this place out of nothin'. Lost her husband on the trail, kept goin', ended up here, and decided we needed an inn. She's a tough one. Got a saying for everything."

Oona re-buttoned the cuff of her night-gown and kept her face averted. She couldn't be blushing. Could she? "And Mr. Williams? He seems like a nice man."

Jenny shrugged. "Pace is all right. He didn't want me on the wagon train, and he wasn't real nice to me on the trail. But he saved my life in the Blue Mountains. Guess we're even."

"And where is he from?" Oona couldn't help herself.

"He never said, I never asked. I don't think even Michael knows. Maybe he don't want us to know. Most ever'one out here has something they'd just as soon forget."

Oh, Oona could top most of them.

"Does he — is he —" She was floundering for sure now. God help her. "To see a man like that not married. It's — unusual."

Jenny shrugged again. "He never said nothin' about that. Some people probably think we're courtin'. We have supper together and we ride on Sundays. But if we are, he ain't told me yet."

If he was — well, Oona had better keep her thoughts to herself. Or not have them in the first place.

"He's the only one I trust with Rebel," Jenny went on. "That's my horse, eighteen hands and black as night. And fast. Knows what I want afore I want it. I got him by chance from a livery stable in St. Joe. He ain't gelded, so when I save enough money, I'm gonna have me a horse farm . . ."

"Is there someone else?" Oona winced at the sharpness of her own tone. What was wrong with her? Pace Williams, that was what.

Jenny was silent for a long time, her breezy chatter dammed up like a stream. "Yeah," she said at last. "They was someone back on the trail. An Injun brave name of White Bear. I — kind of liked him."

Even Oona, with three years in a convent, could read that "kind of liked." "How did you meet?"

"I got sick on the trail, trying to catch up to Michael, and Rebel took me to their camp. White Bear and his folk nursed me. They wanted me to stay, but I had to get to Michael, tell him them thugs were looking for him."

"You could go back." Was Oona insane? If Jenny stayed here and married Pace, maybe it would keep her own mind off the man, which stayed there too much in less than a week.

"I could. But I won't." Jenny hugged her knees tighter, and her voice grew distant. "I ain't good enough for White Bear. I'm a saloon girl, or I was. And he's a good man, the chief's son. He'll be chief someday. He was nice to me. Real nice. Ain't never forgot him. But best leave things as they lay."

"Mr. Williams?"

"Pace knows what he'd be getting."

Jenny stopped and went still, listening as the building creaked in the wind. And she sighed. "*Them,* again." She threw on a wrapper and headed for the door.

Oona followed, her bare feet tender against the rough plank floor.

Jenny charged down the hall to Molly's gun case, grabbed a shotgun, and pounded through the kitchen to the back deck. Her voice carried across the settlement. "Simon Merrill, Bobby Foster, Georgie Davis, you get your sorry selves away from this here hotel now. Iffen you want food you can come back in the morning and pay for it. Or tell your mothers to feed you." She fired several shots into the night, shots answered by the thump of feet scampering away.

Molly's head poked, turtle-like, from her bedroom door. "Didn't hurt them, didja?"

Jenny carefully placed the gun back in the rack. "Nope. I never do. But our back fence is startin' to look like a strainer."

Molly snorted. "What can't be cured must be endured. But we ain't got to endure this. I'm getting a lock for the larder."

"Next time, I'm keepin' them boys," Jenny said. "Their mamas can come and get them in the morning."

Oona crawled back to her hard bed and pulled the covers up around her face. She lay shivering in the dark. What kind of place was this?

With luck, she wouldn't be around long enough to find out.

With luck she wouldn't be around long enough to find out.

6

"Mr. Williams, you nurse dat drink all night?"

Pace shrugged and took another sip of his whiskey. "Makes less work for you."

With a shake of his massive head, the bartender, Ed Petersen, turned to refill a glass for a more enthusiastic customer. "Less money, too," he mumbled.

Pace's one whiskey per night was one whiskey more for Petersen's cash box. And Petersen did a fair business among the lonely loggers.

"Mr. Williams, you never get drunk," Petersen said with a kind of reluctant admiration.

"I spent most of the 1830s drunk. Drunk don't solve nothin'." It didn't bring people back or change what had taken them away. Drunk or sober, gone was gone.

"How you stop?" Petersen's face was alive with professional curiosity.

"I got a job as a scout, and then a wagon master. You got to have a clear head when you're lookin' after two hundred people."

Petersen nodded doubtfully. "I *tink* so. More people be like you — but then I don't make money."

The barkeep was a tall Swede who'd done almost as many jobs as Pace. Nobody knew why he'd taken to bartending, and nobody asked. He had a prison tattoo on one forearm. He carried an air of danger. Pace was the only man in the settlement who wasn't a little afraid of Petersen. Pace and Mike, but then Mike never set foot in the saloon. Another casualty from his new wife — and his new religion.

Petersen's shoulders were broad and his head bumped every doorway in town. His hair, so blond it was almost white, hung past his shoulders. He bound it with a leather thong. He looked like one of the Norse gods in the fairy stories "she" used to read to them. But thoughts of "her" lead to thoughts of them.

He looked around, squashing that line of thought. The room smelled of sawdust, spilled liquor, unwashed men. The kind of room he'd spent half his life in. When had this become not enough? He could get a woman for the night down in the section of town nobody talked about. When had that become more trouble than it was worth?

Tonight, Moses Jackson, the town's only colored man, was on duty, cleaning glasses, wiping down the tables. Pace nodded to him. Jackson was Mike's friend. Seemed like a decent sort. Pace didn't mind coloreds. If a man stuck it out on the trail and made it to Oregon, he deserved to have a chance here.

Victor Curtis, foreman at the Tucker's Creek logging camp, dealt cards at the table in the far corner. The flush of alcohol made his olive skin look even darker. He was mean enough sober, pushing his horse to the limits of exhaustion, brawling with other loggers about a stand of trees or a spilled drink. Most of Hall's Mill liked it fine when he stayed out at the camp. And his men weren't much better. They were all in town tonight for whatever reason. When they descended on Hall's Mill the mamas kept their children at home, and the decent men found some place else to be that wasn't the saloon.

"I hope he win," Petersen said in an undertone.

"Me, too," Pace murmured back. "For everyone's sake."

Curtis took a puff of his cigar. It slipped

from his hand and rolled across the plank floor. He snapped a finger. "Boy! Pick it up, won't ya?"

Jackson put down the tray he was carrying. His face was a smooth brown mask. Head bent, he started to cross the room.

But Pace got to the cigar first, picked it up by the end, and handed it to the logger. "Best be careful, Curtis. This place is so dry it'd go up like a campfire."

Curtis scratched at the mass of hair at his open collar and belched before scowling his answer. "Colored boy coulda got it."

Pace stretched a little, showing his full height. That usually got 'em. "I don't see no 'colored boy.' I see a man trying to do his job. Let it go, Curtis."

Mean drunk, mean sober. Didn't make no difference with this one.

Curtis focused on Pace. The man seemed to get sharper when he drank, instead of the opposite. "You're friends with the Mick, ain't ya? Say, his wife's a looker."

"Tell him that and you'll be on crutches."

Was it worth a fight? Not yet. And Mike was capable of defending his wife.

Pace had enough to drink for one night. He wiped his mouth on his sleeve, nodded to the lumbermen in various stages of stupor, and hoped they made it home all right, but they weren't his problem. He had to make an early start tomorrow, a delivery all the way over to the coast. " 'Night, Petersen. See you tomorrow."

Because he most likely would.

Pace stopped by the bar most every night after Jenny had hauled off the supper things. Better'n being alone in his drippy cabin. He knew how to read. The nuns at the orphanage had seen to that, but he'd never been a reader, and it wasn't as though Hall's Mill had a library like Mr. Carnegie helped to build in the bigger cities back East. Sometimes, Mike and Caroline invited him over, but he wasn't one to push. Better to come in here, nurse one drink, and talk about nothing. Or listen to nothing. Leastways, there were people here, in this frame shack with one counter and three splintery tables. One drink did him fine. Coffee would be better, but Petersen's coffee wasn't fit to drink even by Hall's Mill standards.

And at least he'd been there tonight to help Jackson out. World was hard enough without being judged by skin color.

He'd never been lonely before. If anything, there had been too many people around. But he had time on his hands in Hall's Mill. Time and the example of his best friend's happiness.

Mike joined him as he loped across the silent town. "You done for the day?"

"Ed ain't closed yet, but I had enough. Curtis is there."

Mike nodded. There wasn't much to say about Curtis. "I thought I saw a light in the stables, but 'twas nothing. I'll walk the rest of the way with you." Mike matched his stride. "Caroline was askin' if you wanted to come to supper tomorrow. She's stewin' up a mess of prairie chickens I shot, and she remembered you liked that on the trail."

Pace drew a deep breath and blessed Caroline Pierce O'Leary Moriarty. "Course I will." Maybe Oona would be there. Maybe she wouldn't. But it was one less night in the bar.

A scream ripped through the silence of the night. Pace skidded to a stop. His hand went automatically to his holster. He tried to pinpoint the direction the scream had come from. Behind the hotel . . . not good. Not good at all.

" 'Tis Oona." Mike spun around.

They broke into a run.

Two figures struggled on the platform outside the kitchen door. The man was tall, with a thatch of reddish hair that stood up like a rooster's comb. Harry Bennett, one of Curtis's gang.

"C'mon, honey." Bennett's voice drifted back to him. "It's just a little kiss. I ain't gonna hurt you." But the hard hands at Miss Oona's waist told another story.

Pace would know that thick black braid anywhere. He'd thought about it every night this week.

Mike jumped in first, wresting Bennett from Oona. "Leave her alone. Now!"

Pace's brain shut down. Nothing existed but the three of them . . . himself, Bennett, and Oona Moriarty. He pounded up the wooden platform, the hotel's loading dock, tried to talk but nothing came out, leastways nothing that could be recognized as words.

Mike had peeled Bennett away from his sister and was holding the logger off with one arm. "Do not ever," he rasped, "touch my sister again. Or any other woman in this town. I mean it, Bennett."

Pace tackled Bennett with a roar. He heard heavy footsteps, the sound of men running, but it didn't matter. He was dimly aware of Miss Moriarty straightening her clothing, a white blur to his side, before he punched Bennett in the stomach.

"What's it to you?" Bennett gasped. "She ain't your woman."

"She's a woman. That's enough," Pace said.

Bennett pushed Pace away, but Pace wasn't finished. He delivered a hard right to Bennett's jaw. Bennett howled, reared back, and tried to punch Pace in return. Pace slipped behind the logger and twisted his arm behind him. Bennett had honed his muscles in the woods — but Pace had fought for his life for nineteen years. He threw the younger man to the ground and knelt on him, pounding his head against the boards, unaware of anything except the need to stop Bennett. Even if Bennett was done.

Mike yanked him off the moaning lumberman. " 'Tis enough, Pace. What's got into you, man?" Mike shoved him against the back wall. "Faith! And you don't need to kill him!"

Pace's breath came in short gasps. He craned his neck around Mike, who still had him pinned to the wall with one hand. Nathan Wilkins and Joe Foster, village men, with nightshirts stuffed into their denims, knelt on either side of the logger, examining his wounds. And there were plenty of wounds. The moonlight illuminated the streaks of reddish-black liquid on the porch boards.

Wilkins looked up at Mike. "We've got to get him inside."

"Not in my place." Molly Davis, the hotel owner, stood behind him clutching a wrapper, with her gray hair hanging in snakes. "Nobody hurts one of my workers. Take him down to the bar. Petersen will have whiskey, and he'll need it."

Wilkins and Foster left, supporting Bennett like human crutches.

Mike turned to his sister. "Are you all right?"

She hadn't cried out again, hadn't cried at all, and her lovely face was still as a winter pond. "I'm all right." She threw a chilled glance toward the departing Bennett. "He was just a nuisance." She turned to go back inside.

Molly put an arm around her, murmured words of comfort.

Jenny picked up the shawl Oona had dropped.

Strange little Sadie, the kitchen girl, patted Oona's arm and made a mewling sound.

But as Jenny held the door, Oona looked back, her gaze searching until she found not her brother, but Pace.

He stared back until she turned away. Would she thank him? Did he even want her to? No.

The moon went behind a cloud and Hall's Mill was silent again, as silent in the dark as only a town where people got up before dawn could be.

Mike was the only one left, and he looked as if he wanted to shake Pace. "What ails you, man? Faith. 'Twas my sister, and I'm not even that angry. I would have taught him a lesson. I think I did. But I wouldn't have tried to kill him. I've never seen you like that."

He knew why he'd lost that control tonight. But it was something he couldn't explain to Mike. And even if he could have, he wouldn't. "Lemme alone," he muttered and shoved his way past his friend. "Just let me go home."

Would this night ever end?

Oona endured having her hair re-braided by Jenny, a blanket draped around her by Molly, the standard cup of tea, again from Jenny, and Molly's stream of insults to the absent Harry Bennett. Molly had managed to come up with two proverbs, "Virtue is its own reward" and "if you milk the cow first, you'll never buy it." Oona was still puzzling that one out.

Even Sadie, the little mute girl, had brought her a cold compress for her head.

Oona had smiled at them all, waved them away, insisted she was fine, that he hadn't hurt her. Because, really, what else could she do? She'd sent everyone else to bed, smiled 'til her cheeks hurt, and told them it was nothing. Now she sat alone in the dining room, staring out through the one window to the blackness of this night. Because it wasn't nothing.

Bennett's hand at her breast, his meaty lips on hers brought it all back. The spring of her eighteenth year, the stone barn, Squire Hawthorne's son taking what he felt entitled to . . . or trying to. Blood spilled on a sunny morning that set in motion the whole chain of events: the convent, Michael's exile, the scattering of their family. This Bennett, he was nobody. But the feelings the incident brought back . . . those were real.

Pace Williams. Who was he, anyway? She knew the easy answers: friend of Michael's, wagon master, jack of all trades. Tall, dark, lean in a good way. A slow grin and those hooded brown eyes that held a flicker of warmth when they looked at her. But who was the man driven by violence who had come to her defense tonight?

When he looked at her, sure, and it pierced to her very soul, it made Oona tremble, even after all she'd been through. But she couldn't look away. 'Twas like he'd been waiting for her, and she for him. As if he knew her — across an ocean and a desert and two mountain ranges. Across the mannered minuet of life in Old Ireland to the no-holds-barred American West.

And Mr. Williams' anger was real. Would he have killed Bennett? Would blood be shed again because of her?

Bennett's hand at her breast, his meaty lips on hers. But that wasn't the worst of it. Bennett didn't matter. He was a pawn in a greater game.

It would have to stop somewhere, and it was up to her. As she got up and headed to her room, she felt the weight of her twenty-two years.

Nice if he'd had another whiskey.

Pace didn't light the lamp, just fumbled his way into bed. Cabin wasn't big enough to get lost in. He clasped his hands behind his head as he pondered the puzzle of Oona Moriarty.

She hadn't cried, not after that first scream, and as the women fussed over her, she had acted . . . what? Almost as though she didn't want to be bothered. Like she had something bigger on her mind, bigger than what Bennett wanted to do.

Pace was sure that Bennett's ultimate goal had to be the worst thing that could happen to a woman. He'd never forced a woman, never had to, but he'd seen the fallout and sometimes had to clean up the remains, punishing the offender with whatever justice was available, comforting the sobbing woman. But there she was, looking down her nose at Bennett like some ancient Irish queen.

Well, heaven help the man who tangled with this one.

Heaven or Pace.

And the look she'd given him as the women mother-henned her back into the building. A searching look, one that stripped his defenses to his core, a look that said on some level she knew him. *Knew* him.

It was the one thing he'd avoided as he'd cast his lot with loneliness. He didn't pretend to understand women, and until now, he hadn't wanted to. Be with one a month, a week, a night, and then cut them loose. It had worked for nineteen years. And he couldn't lose control again.

He would have to be careful. He couldn't afford to be found out. And if he gave in to this Oona, his defenses would go down faster than one of these tacky buildings.

64

If they came for him, their anger simmering after nineteen years, they would hurt her too.

Oona Moriarty was a luxury he couldn't afford.

7

Oona stood in a shadowed niche of the livery stable as dawn's light flooded the main aisle. The last barn she'd been in had been *that* barn. She clutched the doorframe as memory rushed in. No, she'd never be completely free of that day.

But this was a new barn and a new world, especially just after dawn. A shaft of sun highlighted the dust motes. *Pretty.* She could hear the town waking up outside, the rich voices of men in lighthearted squabbling as they went off to work their claims. The tramp of their boots, the neighing of their horses, the pattering of smaller feet as a child ran after them with a forgotten lunch pail. A new day. Even here, it was invigorating.

And Michael's voice rose and fell in lilting rhythm. "You're a lovely thing, yes you are," he crooned as he groomed one of the horses. "What a good girl! Stand still now and I'll have a bit of a treat for you when we're done."

Her heart lightened, and she smiled.

Michael had always had a way with horses. And women. And people, with the exception of the English who ruled their small country. They hadn't been impressed by Michael's charm.

But she needed those skills now. She stepped from the shadows to where Michael brushed a dainty, little brown and white mare.

He turned at her footsteps, and his face lit up as only Michael's could do. "Look, Oona. Isn't she fine? I'm thinkin' of buying her for Caroline. She'll need her own mount when we get our place, and Patsy here is a sweetheart. 'Course Caroline could handle something a lot stronger. She's a wonderful rider. You should have seen her keep up with Dan and me . . ."

Oona suppressed a sigh. He bragged about Caroline every chance he got. Nice that he'd found someone, and someone so apparently flawless. She liked her sister-in-law, but it wasn't why she'd come here. "How is Caroline?"

"She's well, thank you. And about to change jobs. The men who have children here formed a school board, so they have, even though this is not part of the States just yet, and they asked her to teach."

"That's wonderful!" Anything that would civilize this place was wonderful.

"The store job will be coming open. Maybe you could take it. See Annie Two Stars. She's the owner."

"I've never worked in a mercantile . . ."

"This one? You only need to be able to read, write, and cipher. Which puts you ahead of half of the town." He led Patsy back into her stall and brought out Jenny's Rebel. "Jenny likes to care for her own horse but she can't when she works the breakfast shift."

Oona handed Michael the platter, still warm and towel-covered. "Shortbread." She hoped her voice didn't betray her. Hoped he couldn't sense the pounding of her heart. "I got up early to make it. For you."

Michael accepted the plate and put it on an overturned barrel. "Thank you. It smells wonderful. Sure and I've missed your short-bread . . . ." He reached for the curry comb and began to brush Rebel, whose coat already gleamed like black satin. "So. Oona. What do you want?"

"I — I —"

Michael grinned. "Oons." He used her childhood nickname. "Sure and you've never baked for me in your life without a reason. What do you want?"

No way out. Like most of her life.

"I want you to come back to Ireland with me, join one of the groups, and help me get revenge for Kevin's death. I want to kill the landlord who had him murdered." She wished she could have enjoyed seeing his mouth fall open, hearing the intake of breath.

He dropped the curry comb, and his voice shook as he bent to retrieve it. "You're daft, woman."

"Not so." She put a hand on his rough flannel sleeve and withdrew it when he shrank back. " 'Tis why I'm here. You need to help me avenge Kevin — yes, and all of them. They tossed our house. They killed Ma. Tom and the others are lost, mayhap forever. It has to stop."

"I can't, Oona. I'm a married man now."

"Caroline can wait. Or she can go with us. She can — she can cook or something. Please, Michael. This is your family." She'd never begged him for anything before. Not even when he'd turned her over to Tom, the journey that ended behind convent walls. Not even then.

Michael exhaled, kept a firm grip on Rebel's lead, and sank onto a hay bale. "So

69

is Caroline. Did ye have to cross an ocean and a continent? Why did you not ask Tomeen? Aside from the fact that it's murder, I mean."

"I told you. I couldn't find him. And Tom wouldn't do it. You know how he is."

Their oldest brother was slow. Not dim-witted in any way, but he moved slowly, like the changing seasons, the stars in their courses. The farm work Michael chafed at fit Tom like his own skin. And for an Irishman, he didn't fight all that much. Michael, two years younger, had had to defend Tom in school.

Tom would not help. If he had wanted revenge on the system that had torn his family apart, wrenched him from farming, and made him homeless, he would have gotten it by now. Or died trying.

No, only Michael would suit. Michael was all she had.

She had delivered her trump card, but Michael was not impressed. He looked up at her, his blue eyes — the Moriarty eyes, mirrors to hers — dark and troubled. "Oona, you can't beat the English. They always win. If I hadn't left Ireland the way I did, I would have left another way. Or in a coffin. Tom survived all those years because he learned to take it, to work around them.

70

I could never do that."

She knew that. Michael would get himself noticed, for good or ill. It was what he did.

But she couldn't give up yet. She couldn't. The losses were his blood too. She could argue anyone into a hole. Da had teased that she should have been a barrister. But Michael was good too; she'd give him that.

Michael got heavily to his feet. He began to brush Rebel's already shining coat. "And you seem to forget there's a price on my head in dear old Eire. Charlie Kennedy and Aidan Kelly died in the Blue Mountains trying to get my scalp. Do you think Hawthorne's given up, just because he's lost two thugs?"

She knew the story by now. Jenny had given her a breathless account of how Hawthorne's hired guns had tracked Michael to America, followed him across the plains, caught up with him in the Blue Mountains. How the secret of the real killer had come out. How the two men had lost their mean little lives in a showdown and shootout.

"And it would be murder," Michael finished, and she knew he'd been saving his trump card for last. "Oons, I haven't had a perfect life. Far from it. I've killed, sure I have — but every time was in self-defense, or in defense of someone else. I can't kill for revenge."

Easy for him to say, with his sweet little wife and the promise of a farm, his own farm, in this brave new world. A farm the English couldn't take from him.

But she'd had three years, four if she counted New York, to hone her arguments. " 'Tis not revenge," she pointed out. " 'Tis justice."

Michael finished brushing Rebel and led the great black beast back into his stall. "It won't bring them back. It won't fix a thing. Oona, the best thing we could do for our kin is to find the ones who are left and get them out of there. Caroline and I want to save enough money to find them. And send for them. Caitrin. The children. Tom. Get the lot of them over here where they can be free. Once the farm turns a profit, we're sending for them."

"Tom will not come. And if he doesn't, the children won't either."

"He will come. Tom is no fool."

There would be no help from Michael. And she thought she knew why. "It's that finding religion of yours, is it not?"

Michael exhaled. His words were deliberate, as though he'd given this speech many a time. "It's not a religion. I gave my life to

Jesus Christ. I made Him Lord and Master. But since you ask, the Bible does say that the Lord claims vengeance as His own. 'Tis not our place."

Vengeance. It had driven her across this vast land, searching for one man. Finding Michael, avenging Kevin, the two dreams had gone hand-in-hand. Those words comforted her behind convent walls, sustained her in steerage, helped her endure life as a servant in New York. They'd fueled her when she'd assisted the older couple in driving a skittish pair of oxen across a flooded river. Driven her in the hot days and cold nights, steadied her when she saw bleached human skulls along the trails. Who would she be now without it? "Then I'll do it myself." She reached for the plate of shortbread.

Michael whisked it out of her reach. "I'm not going, and neither are you. You'd get yourself killed. I can't let that happen."

"You can't stop me."

"I'm the head of the family, so I am. At least, in this country."

"I wish I'd known that when I was working for strangers in New York or helping them slog across the prairie. I've been taking care of myself for a while, Michael."

"Only because I didn't know you were

here. Don't do this, Oons. Stay here and make a life. It's a growing place." He made a vague gesture, one that she supposed was meant to cover all the opportunities in Oregon Country.

"I'm no farmer, Michael. And neither are you."

Michael ignored that last. He moved the towel, broke off a piece of shortbread and savored it before he grinned at her. "As good as 'tis ever was. Oons, you have a gift."

She turned to go. If she spent one more minute in his company, she wasn't sure what she'd do.

"Oona —"

"I'll leave you to your work."

8

"Outta my way. I got to set this down."

As Jenny lugged another steaming kettle her way, Oona had already drawn back. She rubbed the burn on her thumb, sighed, and dumped the lye into the pot when Jenny was safely out of the way. "This is awful." Oona rubbed the burn on her other thumb.

"Better'n cuttin' up buffalo," Jenny said before she sprinted off.

Oona didn't want to know. Making soap. It was Oona's least-favorite domestic chore. Truly, she'd muck a stable or wash a mountain of dishes rather than stand over this inferno all day. Everything she did now was focused on getting away, just as everything she'd done before was focused on getting her here. Michael wouldn't help. Well, she'd do it herself. Somehow. Even if it meant making soap.

Oona brushed back a lock of her hair that had escaped from the scarf that protected it, and wondered if Caroline would like to trade places. Saturdays were busy at the store. Maybe she'd like a break? No. She was sure she couldn't even talk her compliant sister-in-law into this job.

At least they got to work outdoors, under a sun that struggled through the haze. Farmers' wives and loggers' women bustled in and out of the mercantile on their one day a week in town. What would it be like to live outside Hall's Mill in the lumber camps or on a lonely farmstead? Oona didn't want to find out.

She'd had a taste of the city during her year there, wearing out two pairs of shoes on her half-day off. Free museums and galleries, exotic smells, sights in Little Italy and Chinatown, the vastness and variety of Central Park. The world in one city.

She could go back.

Would she be alone? Or was there a man for her somewhere on this continent? Someone who could fill the void Kevin left? Did she want to find out?

Now, at the edge of the known world, Molly pushed back a graying lock. "We were down to our last bar," she reminded her staff. "An ounce of prevention is worth a pound of cure."

It was better than being dirty. But not

much. Oona dumped in more lye, careful not to let it touch her fingers, and stirred vigorously.

Beside her, Molly pronounced her batch done.

And little Sadie wielded a tin dipper to pour the first, cooled batch into molds.

The smell of the boiling lye was carried across the settlement on a breeze, and Oona thought of Molly's next proverb. Would it be "an ill wind blows no one good?"

A bellow of rage crossed the settlement, followed by children's laughter. The wrong kind of children's laughter, the cruel kind. The three women looked up. Some kind of shouting match was happening on the other side of the square, the convergence of the two unpaved roads.

"I'll go," Oona said to no one in particular. Anything to shuck off this chore. She threw down the wooden stirring paddle, caught up her skirts, and ran toward the commotion.

But another pair of long legs had gotten there first.

"See here. What's all this ruckus?"

The oldest Merrill boy, she thought his name was Simon, shrugged. "We was just teasin' him."

Pace folded his arms and looked down at

them. "Who?"

The most ragged of the boys tossed back a lock of too-long brown hair. Tall for his age, he couldn't have been more than eleven or twelve. He cringed even as Pace laid a hand on his shoulder.

"Me. Simon done took my nickel."

"Did not," the Merrill boy said, and the others murmured agreement. "Lucas, he's a liar!"

"Did, too! An' I ain't!" Lucas made a lunge for Simon Merrill, who slipped out of his hands like a fish.

But Pace, with one hand still comforting Lucas, caught the Merrill boy by the jacket collar.

"Turn out your pockets, Simon."

Oona had been here less than a month, but she'd already pegged the Merrill boy as a brat. He was one of the kids who had too much time on his hands, and prowled the settlement looking for a way to misuse it.

Maybe Caroline's school could corral them when she got it started.

The boy wavered but held on to a shred of defiance. "You ain't my pa."

"No, but I can tell your pa. And who'd you think he'd believe? Turn out your pockets." Pace's voice was calm and unhurried, the voice of a wagon master or a crew boss, two of the jobs he'd told her he'd had. Someone who'd be obeyed. And someone who'd faced down harsher groups than this gang of urchins.

The Merrill boy pulled out the lining of his pockets one by one, and a coin, glinting in the weak sunlight, fell from the last pocket to the earth.

Both boys made a grab for it, but Pace reached it first.

"This yours?"

Lucas nodded.

He turned to Simon. "This his?"

Simon mumbled something.

"Thought so. You boys go on, now. Keep what's yours to yourself, and what's someone else's to them."

They scattered with furtive backward looks.

Lucas scuffed his toe against the ground. "Thank ye, Mr. Williams." His voice was barely above a whisper.

Pace waved away the thanks. "You're from the Barlow Camp, ain't you?"

"Yeah."

"What you doin' in town?"

The boy opened his sweaty, grimy hand to show the precious nickel. "My uncle give me this. It's my birthday. He said go in to town and spend it. Ain't never had birthday

79

money before. Or a birthday."

Pace cupped a hand under his chin as he studied the boy. "Well, Lucas, this means we gotta make up for all them lost birthdays." He dug deep in his own pocket. "Here's a couple more nickels. Mercantile's open. See how good you can do."

Lucas looked from the coins to Pace and back again. At last, he trudged off, still staring at the three coins.

Pace turned, and looked at Oona for the first time. "Uncle's probably sleepin' off a bender and don't want to be bothered. I've been out to Barlow camp a lot."

But his words were only half of what he was saying. His dark gaze held hers, and she shivered inside. Did this man know her? Impossible. They came from two different countries, two different worlds.

And she was going back to one of them. She was. She would avenge her family, get a bit of her own back for all the deaths and her three years in the convent. She wouldn't rest until she'd gotten her due. She couldn't afford to get sidetracked by a cowboy, however handsome or kind. She covered his effect on her with chatter. It had always worked before. "What a kind thing to do. Rescuing him from those boys and then the money. Sure, and he won't forget this."

Williams shrugged. "I like kids. And I was an orphan, like Lucas. You don't see too many nickels."

They stared at each other and at the muddy street. The smell of boiling lye seemed to melt away.

Oona's hand went to her throat. As if she could protect herself. She saw Pace as a boy, a lonely boy, a poor boy. If she'd been there, she would have made sure he had a nickel for every day of his life. And clean clothes and hot food. And love.

He didn't want her pity. She knew that, she already knew he was the proudest man she'd ever encountered. Things had happened to him, things he wouldn't voice to anyone. How did he make it through the day? No, he wouldn't want her pity, and she didn't have a name yet for the other thing she could offer. She was shivering for real now. What was happening to her?

Pace doffed his wide-brimmed hat, his expression veiled again. "Got to go, Miss Oona. Got a delivery to do."

She wanted to run back to the hotel fore-yard and stir her cauldron like a mad-woman. Instead, she held her ground.

He was Jenny's. Wasn't he?

But what a fine father he'd make.

Pace shivered as he watched the boy go with the lumpy gait of someone whose shoes didn't quite fit. Well, he'd done the right thing, though he didn't know what good it would do. Get the kid used to nickels and he'd be upset when they stopped coming.

The kid reminded Pace of himself, tall for his age, lanky. But at the orphanage, Pace had been better dressed and, he wagered, better fed. Kid was too thin. Pace hoped he'd buy a cookie or something instead of junk.

He turned to find Oona Moriarty watching him with those big blue eyes like Mike's but thoughtful where Mike's usually weren't.

Did she feel sorry for him?

The one thing he never wanted. Especially from someone like her. No, he didn't want pity from her.

"We're making soap," she said.

"Then you'd best get back to it, Miss Oona."

9

Pace seldom had trouble sleeping. In his varied career, he'd learned to take rest where he could, just as he'd learned to grab a meal when it was offered, no questions asked. Tonight was different. He tossed on his pallet and didn't know why.

Could be the snow. Though the Klamath Mountains were knee-deep in snow, these foothills usually saw more rain. Not that it didn't get cold, a damp, bone-chilling cold that sent the settlers to coughing over the smoky fires in their shacks. Molly at the hotel made a lot of soup on those days.

Snow. Not as much as he'd seen in the Canadian lumber camp, but enough. He'd known it was coming, sensed it in the frigid air and the sky's peculiar shade of gray. Smelled it even, and he'd not been surprised yesterday when the first fat flakes began to drift down from that leaden sky.

The total snowfall was three and a half

inches. With great ceremony, Caroline had measured it with a yardstick. The kids in her new school went wild, throwing handfuls of the stuff and sliding through it. The snow was so light that their mothers swept it off their stoops and then paused with brooms in their chapped hands, smiling as the young'uns tumbled like puppies. Tonight, the clouds parted to reveal an almost-full moon. The red-cheeked, exhausted children were tucked away.

And Pace was as wide awake as he could get. He slept in his clothes, changing them out in the morning. One had to on the trail. Had to be ready at a moment's notice. He didn't even own a nightshirt. Now he swung his legs to the floor, not too hard when his bed was on the floor, and stuck his feet into a pair of boots. A flannel shirt over his flannel shirt would do, cold didn't bother him. Lots of things worse than being cold.

The powdery snow sparkled in the moonlight as the village slept. A weeknight, even the saloon was quiet by now. The buildings were dark except for one light down at the livery stable. Mike working late?

He walked to the bridge, leaned over the split-log railing, watched the cold churning water of the creek, and knew that the village wouldn't be peaceful for long. He'd always had a sixth sense for danger, knowing when his company was in trouble. Mike had marveled at it. Wasn't hard if you stopped talking long enough to hear the wind, sniff an odor, notice a broken branch. But Mike never stopped talking.

Something was wrong, or would be. Pace knew it as well as he knew he was in Oregon Country, that Mike was married to Caroline, and that Jenny made good pie. Someone or something was in for a hard time. And he couldn't protect them because he didn't know what it was.

Here she came in the moonlight, Mike's sister, as crazy as Pace for being outside. Her homespun blouse and skirt, faded by many washings, looked almost white, and a creamy shawl added to the illusion. Her only color came from her red lips and coal-black hair. She could have been an angel.

Yeah, an angel who dunked him and Mike in a horse trough and pulled a gun on Pace. Then there was the little business of killing someone.

They had not spoken, not even a hello, since the business with the Barlow kid.

He hadn't wanted to be thanked. And he couldn't think of what else to say to her. Better come up with something, fast. "Couldn't sleep?" he asked as she drew closer. Well, he'd done better.

Oona Moriarty raised one elegant shoulder. "I'd say it was something I ate, but since I helped cook dinner, that would implicate me."

She could make a word do a back flip, like Mike could, and come out sounding better when it was back on its feet. She joined him at the railing.

They watched the moon's shimmering swath broken up by the fast-flowing creek, like a moving cracked mirror.

"I wanted to thank you for helping me. With Mr. Bennett. I mean, against Mr. Bennett."

"Wasn't anything." It was, but she didn't have to know that. Ever. "Are you settling in?" he asked instead. *Smooth, Williams.*

"As much as I want to be. There wasn't much to settle with. I took Caroline's place at the mercantile, and I'm still helping Molly in my free time."

"You could stay." Well, why shouldn't she? Join their ragtag group, throw in her lot with Hall's Mill. There were worse places. And she made this place look some better. "The store will keep you busy. This is a growing town — them forests out there are pure gold. Hall's Mill wasn't even here five years ago."

"Maybe I will," she said lightly. "I haven't decided yet."

But where else was there to go, to be? Surely not back to the States. Nobody in his right mind wanted to make that trip again, especially no woman. Surely not back to Ireland, for the same reasons and more. He wasn't normally chatty with women, but this one intrigued him. Too much. "Must be different from Ireland. What was it like in the convent?"

Oona stared down at the rushing, foam-tipped water. "It's a good life for those who are called," she said at last. "It was a safe place for me to hide. And it's not that I wasn't religious. I just asked too many questions. There's a big marble entrance hall, and I scrubbed it at least once a week. I had to do it on my knees, as a penance, for talking out of turn or being late to chapel or leaving a fork out of the drawer. And the funny thing was, I never confessed my real sin."

Something rose in him, a desire to plead her cause. To whom? "That was self-defense, far as anybody's told me. Every man I ever killed was self-defense. It happens."

"I don't want to get in Michael's way. Him with his new wife, and all. But as long as I stay with Jenny, 'twill be fine. We're getting on well."

Pace didn't want to talk about Jenny. Not tonight. Not at all.

"Have you seen her horse?" Oona prattled on. "Rebel. She talks about him all the time. Oh, and sure you have, I would think."

Rebel. The coal black stallion Jenny had helped herself to back in St. Joe. The horse that had saved her life twice and almost cost her it once, on a desolate crag in the Blue Mountains. Rebel, fast and sure, who knew what his rider needed, sometimes before the rider did.

"I seen 'im. We take a horse ride every Sunday." He needed to know more about Oona. "Do you have a skill, a trade?"

"I guess I'm a cook. That's what I did in the manor house, helped in the kitchen. I can cook, clean, take care of children. I can read and write." She flashed that Moriarty grin. "For now, it's the mercantile. But I'm sure I'll find something to do." She lifted her face to his, not that there was that far to lift. She was a tall girl, and she started to say something. But it died on her lips as she looked up at him.

He'd never gotten this close to her. Never dared.

Though he couldn't see their blueness, her eyes were wide in the moonlight. She

88

had a dusting of freckles on her nose. Her lips were full. But he could see that under the chatter and bustle, all that Moriarty-ness, she was tired. Bone-weary. And lovely. And she was the danger, at least for tonight. "I should be going." He still wasn't tired. But he wasn't sure what he'd do if he stayed.

Oona moved a little away from him, nodded in that queen-like way she had. "I think I'll stay out a bit longer. Good night, Mr. Williams."

He hesitated, remembered that winter night a few weeks before. No bachelor loggers in town tonight, it was a weeknight and late, but still. "You'll be all right alone?"

"Mr. Williams, I've been alone for a while."

Oona watched Pace Williams amble off. A nice figure of a man, and a nice man. Jenny was lucky, or would be lucky if she ever said yes. Pace and Jenny dined together every night, and now she knew they went riding every Sunday. Everyone said it was only a matter of time.

What would it be like to have a man like Pace by her side? For so long it had always been Kevin. For three years in the convent, it had been Kevin she'd dreamed of, Kevin, and their reunion. Kevin, who made it impossible for her to take those final vows.

She stared at the moon on the water and knew that sleep was still a long way off. Ma would have said, "You need your rest." Well, there was nothing here she needed her rest for. She'd worked all her life. She could do her store job in her sleep and help Molly around the edges. A continent and an ocean separated her from anything that mattered.

And Michael wouldn't help.

On snowy days back home Ma would gather them around the fire, with warm bannock bread and steaming cups of tea, and she'd tell stories. Though Ma was as Christian a woman as could be found in the village, she knew all the old myths and legends, battles and banshees, shape-shifters and warrior queens. Her voice dropped to a thrilling whisper when she spoke of the Morrigan, the female harbinger of death.

Oona loved the story of Finn McCool, how when he was hunting one day, he came upon a fawn. His hounds wouldn't let him kill it, and he took it home. That night the fawn turned into a beautiful woman, Sadbh. Enchanted by a druid, she was safe as long as she stayed in Finn's territory, the Dun. They married. But when Finn went off to battle, the druid tempted Sadbh out of the Dun, and she was never seen again.

Like Kevin. When Oona came out of the convent, he was gone. No enchantment there, just his wanting things to be different. Different from being Irish in Ireland.

She remembered a summer day, the colors more vivid in memory — the green grass, blue sky, and flowers paint box-bright. She and Kevin sprawled on their backs in a meadow high above the village. They'd held hands, though their bodies were decorously apart. Oona was a good girl. Good enough, anyway.

Sweet Kevin, with his golden curls and the laugh that caused even strangers to turn around with smiles. He'd been her brothers' friend first, around so often villagers called him the "blond Moriarty." Nobody was surprised when he started calling on Oona.

She remembered propping herself on one arm, about to tease him about something, when he'd turned to her, his gray eyes sober for once. " 'Tis something you should know."

"Kevin, you proposed to me when we were six."

"No, not that." His quick smile faded. "I've joined a group."

In their country, it could only mean one thing. "You're in the underground." She drew her hand away. The sun went behind a cloud. The colors faded. She reached for her shawl.

"I had to. Oona, there has to be change. We can't live like this. 'Tis not what I want for us — or for our children."

She remembered the church bells chiming three, a crofter urging his sheep along. The smells of summer, peat and manure, animals and flowers, and sweet, long grass. The home she'd never wanted to leave. "We'll do fine," she'd said. "I have a good job. You have a good job. We needn't have that much to do with the English. It's not like the old days."

Well, some of them.

"If we leave them alone, they'll leave us alone." She'd say it until she believed it.

Kevin sat up, ran a hand through his yellow curls. His voice was the voice of a stranger. "So you've forgotten Maeve, then."

Maeve, his younger sister, ten or twelve then, a young woman now if she'd lived, though Oona had no way of knowing. Cheerful and friendly as she'd moved about the cottage with the crutch Kevin had carved. Bringing tea, kneading bread. A relative's hearth was the only home Maeve would know since Hawthorne Senior's horse had spooked one Market Day, kicked out and sent the youngest O'Halloran girl sprawling. Her leg had never set right; they couldn't afford a doctor. Maeve was pretty enough with Kevin's golden curls and gray eyes, and she was a smart enough child. But few men would be able to look beyond the crutch. A woman needed to be strong — as strong as her man — to live the life of an Irish tenant.

"She'll always have a home with us," Oona remembered saying.

"That makes up for nothing. Hawthorne didn't offer to pay for a doctor. Didn't even ask after Maeve. Oona, it's got to stop."

From then on, she'd pretended not to know about his clandestine meetings. She would have gone on pretending, right into their marriage, but for her own attack by — and on — a Hawthorne. Michael and Tomeen had worked fast, stashing her in the convent. When she came out three years later, she'd found Kevin had died, the result of a raid gone bad; her family scattered, and Ireland still Ireland.

She had loved Kevin fiercely, his hearty laugh, his gentleness with her and his crippled sister, his intelligence. She had loved him since childhood.

Kevin.

Maeve, probably dead.

Ma, dead in a ditch after the eviction.

Caitrin, who'd be seventeen now, lost somewhere between the village and Uncle Eamon's.

Orla disappeared into poverty, abuse, or both. No one had seen Orla since her marriage off the estate. Tom and the "littles." Had they survived?

Her brother Dickie, dead from pneumonia before any of this happened. Michael, for a while. And three years of her own life, lost forever to that convent. She tallied the things the English had taken from her.

Did Pace Williams know about loss? Oona thought he did. She'd love to be the one to make him laugh again. But not 'til her business was settled. And besides, he was earmarked for Jenny.

"Kevin," she whispered into the silver night. "I'll take care of it, so I will."

Pace walked in the opposite direction until his breathing finally slowed. Oona Moriarty. He didn't even know her yet, and he already knew she was trouble. Could he go back, invite her to his lonely cabin? Just to talk? To keep the darkness away? Could he keep it at talk?

Prob'ly not.

He saw a man crossing the square and recognized Mike's long-legged stride. Late night at the livery stable. Drawing into the shadows, he watched as a square of light appeared at the Moriarty cabin, as Caroline's small figure blocked the doorway, as the two silhouettes fused.

Someone to come home to. And there were so many reasons it shouldn't be Oona Moriarty. He couldn't let himself love her. She wasn't staying. He saw it in the faraway look in her eyes. He could never talk this woman into the drudgery that went along with being a farm wife, a ranch wife.

Jenny could live the life of an Oregon settler and then some. Jenny, now there was the kind of wife he needed if he meant to stay. And Jenny knew him, at least as much as he wanted to be known. Jenny could take his mind off Oona. Jenny could take any man's mind off anything.

He would talk to her. Soon.

10

"Mike! Hey, Mike!" Pace hurried to catch up with his friend, as Mike hurried home from the livery stable.

Mike turned, with that big grin of his. "Pace, my man. What can I do for you?"

"Nothin' much. Wondered how Caroline's farin' with the school."

That got Mike talking as Pace had known it would. Didn't take much to get Mike to talk about his wife.

"Well enough." Mike's pace slowed. "The children love her, and there's been no discipline problems. Other than the Wilkins boy, who has more energy than sense. Most of 'em want to learn, she says. I'm thinkin' they were so bored they actually wanted to get back to studyin'. Only thing I don't like is her holdin' it in the hotel dining room. Curtis comes in, drinks coffee while she's teaching. Makes her uncomfortable."

Victor Curtis would make any woman uncomfortable.

"Well, we'll see about buildin' her a school." When had he and Hall's Mill become a "we"? "And . . . Miss Oona? Is she well?" He couldn't have stopped himself from asking. He hoped Mike didn't wonder why. Pace collected information on the feisty Irishwoman, sorted it out in the quiet times on his courier runs. He knew she liked milk in her tea, lots of it; that she'd done something called step-dancing back in Ireland; that dark blue, like her eyes, was her favorite color. While she admitted she wasn't much of a reader, she could tell a story with flair. And he knew that there was something she wasn't telling any of them. If he had to, he could probably pass a test on Oona Moriarty.

In the past, Mike didn't pick up on things like that, and he didn't now. "She is doing well. A born shopkeeper, that one. Annie's glad she was able to take over from Caroline. 'Twas a good move. And she still picks up some work at the hotel, especially on Sundays."

"Is she stayin' on?" Please, don't let his face show anything. There was nothing to show. Was there?

" 'Tis my hope, and Caroline's, too. I wasn't sure in the beginning, but . . ."

Michael shrugged. "She's as well off here as anywhere. We want to see her settled. Then we'll find Tom and send for him and the children. We're savin' for that."

Michael had reached the door of his cabin. "You'll come in and have some supper? 'Tis only stew tonight, but Caroline makes good stew, you'll remember from the trail."

"Naw. Jenny'll be over with my grub." Jenny, whom he was about to court. Jenny, who should have been enough for any man.

"Then come for coffee later. Caroline found more newspapers, news from back east. We can talk about what's been happening."

It beat going to the bar and having his one whiskey, trading meaningless chatter with Petersen and the loggers. Beat going back to his cabin and staring at the leaky walls.

And maybe Oona would be there.

"Sure, Mike. I'll be over."

Pace walked on to his own shack and waved to a couple of acquaintances. Mike was always happy these days, a man on top of the world, living with his Caroline and working with the horses he loved.

Seemed to Pace as if Mike wanted to share his happiness, fold Pace into his little family

98

circle. Caroline wasn't far behind. They had always been generous. Couldn't fault them for that.

And they were sending for Tom and the rest of the crew. If they could find them. Must be nice to have a family, even if it was on the other side of the world.

He'd heard about Thomas, the oldest brother. Heard tales of his and Mike's childhood exploits and how Tom had stepped up to head the family after their father died. How Tom could coax anything out of soil. Tom was a man he'd like to meet. And if they had any more at home like this Oona . . .

He wasn't to think that way. One Oona was too much when he was almost promised to Jenny. But that was part of the problem. He'd never met anyone like Oona Moriarty, and being with Jenny was like being with himself. He looked down at his shirt and jeans, mud-spattered from a day of hard riding. Wouldn't hurt to change. Maybe shave, too.

As Pace left the warmth and light of the Moriarty cabin, Michael's voice followed him. "Don't eat all your cookies on the way home!" Pace tried to think of a clever response, but the door had already closed.

He patted the four raisin cookies in his pocket. Caroline never sent him away with empty pockets.

The town was packing it in, candles being snuffed out in the cabins.

Jenny passed him. "Good night." She was going back to the hotel from their evening at the Moriarty home. A pleasant time with four old friends. Nothing more, no matter how hard they tried.

Oona hadn't been there, and he'd tried to hide his disappointment. Now, as he'd hoped he would, he saw her. No mistaking that tall, slender figure and how she moved. Not for him, anyway. She was cloaked against the damp, her black hair in a loose braid, as she hurried through the darkness toward her room at the hotel. And she carried a small barrel.

"Miss Oona! Let me help you with that." Anything to be near her, even if just for a few minutes. Oh, he was a lost cause.

She started, stumbled, and the barrel fell onto the packed earth.

Pace was on one knee, picking it up, before Oona could respond. He took an idle glance inside and then rocked back on his heels. "Miss Oona —"

"It isn't — I didn't — I paid for them," the woman blurted. "I put money in the

100

cash box, same as everyone else."

"Four *Colt revolvers*?"

The life leached from her face. "Yes." She lifted her chin like some ancient Irish princess. Oh, she was proud, even now. "You won't tell Michael."

That her problem was his problem?

Pace could bargain with the best of them. He'd had to, he'd bargained for his life more'n once. "I won't tell if we can talk a bit. Come on. Let's go back to the store." When she stood still, he put out his hand and trembled when she took it. Her fingers were long and slender, work-worn but still soft. "Come on, Miss Oona."

She was sure-footed in the dark, unlocking the mercantile on one try. By feel only, she found a candle and matches and lit the room. It looked odd in the flickering light, with strange shadows cast by the casks and barrels and most of the corners still dark. He had never been in here at night. No reason to be.

And Oona was even more beautiful in the candle glow, her eyes almost black, her cheekbones highlighted, her lips . . . best not to think that way. He had enough trouble with one woman, and Jenny wasn't even his woman yet.

But he couldn't talk to Oona without

looking at her. That would be too much to ask of any sane man. He folded his arms to keep from touching her and leaned against the counter. "Miss Oona, why do you need four guns?"

She looked away, and the candlelight softened her profile.

Pace braced himself.

"Six. I have two others, so I have, under my bed at the hotel."

"That don't give me the why."

"I am going back to Ireland to avenge my mother's death, my father's death, my fiancé's death, and the loss of our home."

The words fell like stones into the hushed store.

Except for one word, which lodged itself in his heart. "Fiancé." He tucked that one away for further examination. He crossed his arms tighter. "Just how do you intend to do that?"

"There are groups — underground groups, rebel groups. If I can bring them the weapons, they'll help me. I asked Michael to come, but he said no."

Smartest thing Mike had ever done, except for getting Caroline back.

Pace's mouth went dry. Whatever he'd expected, it wasn't this. "So you'd be —

goin' home?" Bad enough if she left, but for this?

She faced him then, her eyes wide and dark, the light playing over her cheekbones and full lips. "Mr. Williams, I have no home. I am going back to Ireland to execute justice."

He didn't like the sound of that. "Miss Oona, you'd be putting yourself at a lot of risk."

"I have nothing left to risk."

Well, he'd seen that look in others, even himself from time to time, the look of someone with nothing to lose. But he couldn't bear it in her.

"And it wouldn't do no good," he plowed on. "You can't fight a whole government, 'specially one as big and mean as that one. You'll — oh, I don't know what you'll do. But it won't end good." Michael's darker stories had shown him that much, and he suspected there were even darker ones Mike didn't share. Pace's heart was pounding. He gestured to a splintered wooden bench. "Let's sit. And you tell me everything."

They sat decorously apart. Good thing it was a long bench.

She told of village fetes and market days, the parish school, Michael's disagreements with the curates and nuns. She talked about

103

a brother, Dickie, frail and gone from them early. She talked about her beloved da, also gone too soon, and how her brother Tom had stepped in to head the family. There was the fiancé, a man called Kevin, and a sister Caitrin, "The bravest person ever."

"No. You are," he blurted, before he'd had a chance to think.

She told him the full story of what had happened with the landlord, details he hadn't heard, and her surprise religious vocation. She told him about Kevin, how she'd warned him against joining the underground, and how he'd paid for it with his life. And she painted a picture of her family, turned out of their cottages to roam the highways until her mother died and the others disappeared into the fog that was Ireland.

She made him see all of it.

What time was it? Did it matter anymore?

Pace cleared his throat. "All right, Miss Oona, here's what I think we should do." When had they become a "we"? "Suppose you put those guns back in the cabinet. Ain't real safe for you to keep all of them, and you can always hold one out for yourself." If she learned how to shoot. "Winter over here, because you can't get through the passes before spring, and you can't do it alone. If you still feel the same way in March, I'll help you out of here." Him and her, alone on a mountain trail. At night. *Sure.* He hurried past that vision. "I can bring you to a fort, and you can get a military escort back east and sail for Ireland from there."

"You wouldn't go east with me?"

"I'm stayin' on here. I'm done with the trail."

Oona pondered his suggestion, and Pace drank in the sight and scent of her. She was as beautiful as Jenny, but Jenny had never stirred these feelings in him. Didn't make no sense. One woman was as good as another, weren't they? Try telling Mike that.

Her gaze had not left his face. He saw a challenge there and a vulnerability — and one slow tear on her perfect cheek. As a man under a spell, he lifted that tear, and the tiny drop of water shimmered on his thumb.

And he lowered his face to hers.

She kissed him back like a starving woman, her arms clinging to his forearms. The dingy shop, the village of shacks, fell away and they were somewhere else, not Ireland, not Oregon, but someplace where they could be just two people. Her lips were soft and his arms tightened around her. Oh, she was nice to hold.

But he didn't know how experienced she was, and he would never take advantage of her. Pace pulled back, with the strength that had helped him through, well, just about everything. He chose his words carefully. "That was nice. Real nice."

"You'll get no argument from me."

She looked up at him with the same challenge and a sort of glow.

Could he? Not and live with himself afterward.

"But we'd best tend to the matter at hand," he finished. "What we came here for."

She handed him a key, and he went to the back room, where she kept Annie Two Stars' inventory of guns. He locked the four revolvers away.

"There. Why don't you bring back one of the two you got, and keep the other? In this country, you need protection."

Oona lifted her chin. "Who would teach me to shoot?"

He wasn't falling into that trap. "Your brother. Any man in the village. Mrs. Moriarty or Jenny, come to think of it — they're both pretty good shots."

Oona nodded. "I will see to it. Good night, Mr. Williams. And thank you." As he turned to go, she caught his sleeve. He half-turned back, and she brushed his cheek with a feather-light kiss, as unsettling in its way as their earlier one.

Oona half-hoped he'd turn back. But Pace's boot heels thumped on the wooden floor, and the door's click spoke of finality.

He was a fine man. Good-looking in a rangy, cowboy sort of way, with that lean build and sharp features. He was as rootless as Kevin had been rooted, a man who'd been everywhere, done everything, with no rules or traditions to hold him back. She'd heard some of his stories, in that measured drawl of his, and longed to hear more.

And his kiss had awakened something in her, something stronger than even Kevin had made her feel. She hadn't wanted to stop. She had wanted more of Pace Williams, in every possible way. A way that made her blush, even in the darkened store.

But he was the West.

And she was the East.

Michael had taught her to ride, a lifetime ago in Ireland. She could learn to handle a gun. Marry a farmer, help wrest a living out of this vast land. But would she ever feel at home here? It was big and raw and wild.

Home was tilled fields and cottages, Mass

and Market Day, the routine that had existed for their people for hundreds of years. One could count on it. One could count on the English taking their share, but if one played their game right, what was left was not too bad.

Michael married. He was coming around. He'd likely make room for her. But was that what she wanted? Spinster aunt, the leavings of someone else's life?

No. She wanted the world that had been ripped from her one bright morning in her eighteenth year, when young Hawthorne had not succeeded in taking her virginity — but she'd lost everything else.

If she hadn't gone into the convent, she would have married Kevin. She couldn't have stopped him from joining the underground. His mind had been made up, but she'd have a child or two to remember him by, and the memory of his love.

Pace drew her in, the first man she'd even looked at since learning of Kevin's death. Her cheeks warmed again as she thought of tonight's kiss. Pace, who belonged to Jenny.

Even though Jenny talked about her horse with more enthusiasm that she did about Pace.

Oona locked the shop and hurried back to her cold bed in the rear of the hotel.

Jenny was asleep, her breathing even, her growing blonde hair spilled out across her pillow. *I'm sorry,* Oona told her silently.

The sooner she left here, got on with her business, the better for everyone. This West was no place for Oona Cathleen Moriarty.

But when she slipped between her own covers, her last thoughts were of the darkened store and one western man's strong arms around her.

11

A rabbit streaked through the underbrush, a blur of gray against the rain-soaked brown leaves, and Pace sat up straighter. He fumbled for his rifle.

But Jenny had already nailed the hare with a single shot. With no wasted motion, she swung herself down from Rebel, tied the hind legs of the rabbit, and fastened the corpse to her saddle horn. Yeah, she was good. She mounted Rebel again and looked over at Pace. "You all right?"

"Why wouldn't I be?"

"You usually outshoot me."

Oh, she must be worried about him to admit that.

Pace shrugged. "Don't matter, there's plenty for both of us." He wheeled around and continued his slow plod down the forest trail.

Theirs would be a good union, if they ever got that far. They wouldn't have to talk.

Jenny was, well, like him. Keeping her scars on the inside, letting the world see only what she wanted. A tough loner who could do anything, because she'd had to.

Mike and Caroline, now, they were as different as night and day. Caroline so dainty and gracious and quiet, Mike big and loud and sometimes stupid. But whatever they had worked for them. Whatever they had? Why did he skip around it? What they had was love.

He didn't love Jenny, not that way, and he doubted that she loved him. But they got on well and they were both alone. People had started out with less.

And he needed someone if he stayed here. This wasn't the trail. He could do it by himself if he had to, but if he had to do it alone, wasn't much point to it. He needed a wife. It was that simple.

If he at least tried to make a life with Jenny, maybe it would clear his mind of black hair and blue eyes and a voice with laughter running through it like a thread. Oona wasn't for him. It would never work. Mike would kill him. And that was just for starters.

A dance was planned for two weeks out, a weddin' shindig to celebrating the union of a town girl and a logger. If he walked in with Jenny on his arm, it would stake his claim before the town. And to Jenny. And to himself.

When they came to a clearing, he paused and took a deep breath of the clean damp air. Time to get it over with. "Wanna go to the dance?"

Jenny's hat had slipped back, and she shaded her eyes against the weak winter sunshine. "Sure. Isn't everyone?"

He counted to ten. "I mean with me."

She waited a beat before answering. Jenny was no fool. Jenny hedged her bets. "I guess so. We'll both be there anyway, won't we?"

He watched another rabbit streak through the underbrush. Was she making this hard? Or was it hard in itself?

"Do you want me to walk over with you?" he asked in measured tones.

Jenny shrugged. "No need. I got to help Molly with the food. I'll see ya over there." She wheeled Rebel around and cantered down a side trail, leaving Pace open-mouthed.

Could he ask Mike how it was done? Not on a bet. Mike would tease him until the day he died and probably beyond. And Mike wasn't himself these days. There was his new religion and some other secret that had him grinning at odd times.

Men had been courting women for centuries. Pace would figure it out.

Oona breezed through Molly's kitchen, grabbing a leftover flapjack from the stack on a platter and devouring it with one hand.

"Don't you want coffee?" Jenny called after her.

"I'll put a pot on at the store," Oona tossed over her shoulder. She could hardly wait to get to the mercantile to begin her day. It was the happiest she'd been in this country, which wasn't saying much.

Caroline was setting up her classroom in a corner of the dining room, and she looked up with a smile. "How do you like running the mercantile?"

"I like it well enough, thank you. It's a nice change from cooking and cleaning. I can read and write and cipher and make change, so that part is easy enough."

She liked the order of the place, after the chaos of the overland journey. She liked matching a bachelor logger with the right flannel shirt, or a new settler with a hammer. And — might as well admit it — she liked serving her customers, hearing all the gossip and the legitimate news, getting a feel for this strange little town. But she wasn't staying.

"I'm glad you were able to take over," Caroline said. "It frees me up to do this. I was a good enough shopkeeper, but teaching children is my calling."

Caroline looked deeply content, her sun-kissed brown hair in a neat bun with a few wisps curling out. Her calico dress was neat on her slender frame, her hazel eyes glowing. Who was this woman who had captivated — and tamed — Michael?

And what was this talk of callings? Oona had never felt called to do anything. Never had a chance or a choice, either in the manor house kitchen at sixteen or in the convent to save her family, or here, where she'd found a stubborn and useless Michael. Was going back to Ireland a calling? It drove her, for certain. It occupied every waking moment and the occasional nightmare during her sleeping ones. It took every spare penny and might result in her death. Was that what a calling did? Did it consume one?

At the sound of a low whistle, Oona froze.

Victor Curtis sipped a cup of coffee at one of the corner tables.

Oona felt her walls go up. Hadn't he learned the lesson from his friend Bennett? She didn't have time for this. Didn't want this.

But Curtis's glance passed over her to

114

fasten on Caroline.

"Wish we'd had teachers like you when I was in school!"

Though Caroline's small hands clenched around a pencil, Oona had to admire her sister-in-law's composure. "It's to be hoped you'd treat her with more respect, Mr. Curtis."

"Yeah, but I bet you could teach me a thing or two." He chuckled, donned his worn hat, and headed for the door.

Oona shifted from one foot to another until she heard his boots thump on the steps. "Does he do that often?"

"Once or twice a week. He comes in for supplies and has breakfast or a cup of coffee. And I'm usually in here setting up before he leaves."

"Michael will kill him."

"He won't, but he'd be tempted. But after what Pace did to Harry Bennett, I don't think Mr. Curtis wants that kind of trouble."

Pace Williams, who had defended Oona and refused any thanks. Who had stood up to a bully, who had shown such rage, but was so gentle with children and animals — and with her. Pace, who was keeping her secret. Because she'd asked him to.

"Caroline, Curtis is a monster." Even Oona, new to the village, had heard tales of how Victor Curtis treated the men who worked for him, and whatever woman wasn't smart enough to get away.

"Yes, but he needs the Lord." Caroline shrugged. "I'll be fine, Oona. I rarely go anywhere alone. I stay close to the settlement, and Jenny and Molly are always in the kitchen."

Well, yes, Oona had seen Jenny in action with the thieving village boys. Pity Oona couldn't convince her to come to Ireland.

Oona could tell Michael herself. Probably should. But it wasn't her business, and she had enough on her hands. Maybe Curtis was just a blowhard and a braggart. Sure, and she'd seen enough of those in her time.

She turned at the sound of light feet on the steps, and Caroline's students burst into the room: the three Dale girls, the younger Merrills and Fosters, lively Zebulun Wilkins, the quieter, shabbier children who rode in from the lumber camps every day, toting their lunches in lard pails. The students' ages ended about eleven or twelve. Anyone older was expected to help with the settling of the land, girls toting water and minding the youngest, boys already out on the claims with their fathers.

"Look, teacher, look at my ribbons!" Six-year-old Ramona Dale preened and tossed her braids.

"They are wonderful ribbons," Caroline said in that voice she reserved for her students, bending to look Ramona in the eye. But she saw something over the girl's shoulder and straightened.

Oona followed her gaze.

Elijah and Deborah Jackson, the only colored children in the settlement, were poised on the threshold.

Their mother stood between them with a hand on each child's back. Dulcinea Jackson was a tall, grave woman who spoke little and always seemed to be looking over her shoulder. Was it her past as a slave? If Oona had to imagine anything worse than Ireland, she guessed slavery would be it.

Today, Mrs. Jackson's dark eyes looked alive. And frightened. "Miss Caroline, you be sure this is all right?" she asked.

Caroline lifted her chin. "Of course, it is. It's a public school, isn't it? Deborah, you sit here with the first graders. And Elijah, I've already seen what you can do. I'll try you in fifth grade."

Zeb Wilkins whooped and gestured for his friend to join him.

And little Deborah was already surrounded by a group of the younger girls, including the beribboned Ramona.

Oona gathered her shawl and slipped out the door. Did Caroline know what she was doing, and risking? It had to be safer than Ireland, but just barely.

12

Pace looked at himself in the shard of mirror he used for shaving.

Hair, all right — he kept it so short he could comb it with a dishrag. Plaid shirt, clean — oughta be. It was his good one. Jeans, clean enough — but boots polished to perfection. He'd do for the wedding dance for Viola and Stephen Miller.

No way he could have gotten out of the wedding supper and barn dance. This community was too small. And truth be told, he didn't mind socializing with these people. They'd crossed this great, vast land and they understood, even the whiners like Mrs. Latham, even that cold fish, Mrs. Wilkins. They knew what it took.

And they liked him. He wasn't sure why.

It was the first party this group of emigrants had planned.

And as good a time as any to stake his claim. For Jenny.

In the process, he would banish the beautiful Irishwoman to a memory. She was leaving anyway, and he was staying. She'd become a fleeting image, awakened by the glimpse of a pair of blue eyes or a swinging black plait. A girl he used to know. Nothing more.

Being with Jenny would help to fade those images. Best he could do, anyway.

Pace drew a deep breath, and the door creaked shut behind him.

A fiddle tuned up somewhere, followed by a guitar. The night was warm with the promise of spring. Residents in groups of two or three streamed toward the lighted barn, while loggers who'd ridden in from the woods tied up their horses.

He located the source of the music, a band cobbled together from anyone in the settlement who owned an instrument. Pace waved to Caroline Moriarty as she arranged cookies on a platter. Michael was hauling chairs and threw Pace one of his big, white smiles.

The newlyweds accepted congratulations under a bower fashioned from branches and festooned with white ribbon. How did women come up with this stuff?

Viola was the oldest daughter of a town family. Steve was a logger. They'd ridden off to the mission to be hitched by Marcus Whitman. Pace could have done it; he had a special license that allowed him to marry people on the trail, like a ship's captain, but he was just as glad they hadn't asked. Hard to join people in holy matrimony when one let God go His way and one went theirs. One of the many things he and Jenny agreed on.

Tonight, the barn smelled of sweet hay and coffee. The stalls had been mucked for the night and the horses fed, and some of them looked on with interest over their half-doors.

And Jenny was there, unloading covered dishes from a basket. She wore a blue dress with a crisp white collar, a little fancier than her everyday duds. She'd tied her hair back with a darker blue ribbon. From a distance, she looked like a schoolgirl. As he came closer, she grinned up at him.

"Hey, Pace."

"Hey, Jen. You look — nice."

And she did, though not in a way to stop him in his tracks.

"Thanks," Jenny said. "Miz Jackson, Moses's wife, lent me this. She made it herself. Not too many tall women in Hall's Mill. Her, me, and Oona."

Don't talk about Oona. "Jacksons comin'

tonight?"

"Prob'ly not. They don't mix much." She lifted a casserole dish, waving away his gesture of help. "I got to set these out. Save me a dance." She flung the words over her shoulder.

Friendship and respect, that would have to do. Better'n most people managed.

"Well, sure, and you clean up well." Oona's voice was laced with laughter.

Silk rustled behind him.

He turned. At the look of her, he understood that life would never be on the same course again.

Oona Moriarty stood in the doorway. Her gown, the color of emeralds, shimmered in the lantern light and hugged her slender waist before spilling out around her. The long, narrow sleeves ended in some kind of frilly stuff. Her mass of black hair was captured in a loose knot at the nape of her neck, a few strands curling around her flushed face.

His heart began to pound. He couldn't have moved if he'd wanted to.

And the mischief in Oona's blue eyes gave way to something else.

"Mr. Williams," she said quietly.

"Miss Oona. You look — you look —"

He had never been good with words.

Wasn't likely he'd start now.

"I hope you like my dress. I've been working on it all week, so I have — something nice for my first dance in the West." Oona, a Moriarty to her bones, covered the awkwardness with chatter. She touched a fold of the skirt. "I already had the cloth. The casket-maker I hitched a ride with gave it to me. 'Twas left over from a coffin lining."

She was resourceful; he'd give her that. And jaw-dropping beautiful, especially in a dance dress the color of emeralds.

The fiddles and guitar broke into a lively tune. She stood beside him. He smelled her hair and her skin, soap and some scent like flowers. He shouldn't. But Jenny was still busy with the food — and here was Oona Moriarty smiling up at him, with humor and just a trace of fear in those dark blue eyes. She was scared. Scared of an old dance.

He held out his arms, and Oona moved into them.

She fit like a glove, tall enough but not too tall, slender but not too slender. As if she'd been carved for him. He smelled her sweet hair, and his heart set to pounding again. His arm tightened around her waist. *Breathe, Pace. Only way you're gonna get through this.*

"You dance very well, Mr. Williams." She

tilted her smiling face up to his. "Where did you learn?

He swung her, a little too forcefully, around the slow-moving Mr. and Mrs. Wilkins. "At the orphanage." He'd been eleven, a kid with a hard shell already forming. But "she" had seen past that shell.

Pace held Oona closer, whirled with more force than necessary until the green skirt swirled around her, until a laughing crowd made room for them and Oona's cheeks bloomed like roses.

Could he tell her? All of it? No. And he'd never wanted to tell anyone more. Wouldn't do no good. Water under the bridge, an ugly bridge. But he couldn't stop. Something about this woman stripped him bare of defenses. "It was a girl," he said at last. "At the orphanage. An older girl. Sh-she looked a little like you."

"Did she now?" Oona teased, but her laughter died as she looked up into his face.

"She was beautiful. Just like you."

He was holding her too tightly, but she didn't pull away, and the expression in those blue eyes softened, deepened. "Was she now," she repeated more softly. And then, "I think our dance is done."

He stayed away from Oona for the rest of the evening. He danced with Jenny more than once, Caroline, and two or three other safe matrons.

Jenny was serving, laughing and joking with the other women. Good, she was making friends.

So he sat supper with the Moriartys.

Caroline picked at her food, and Michael couldn't stop grinning.

Well, they couldn't fool him, and he was happy for them. A child on the way. If he couldn't be a pa he'd be an uncle, and a good one.

Oona did well for herself, sought after by most of the young bucks from the Ames camp, eating dinner surrounded by them. Women were scarce around the lumber camps, and the men all had a good reason for being there. Oona was popular.

Pace heard her laughter, saw the swirling green skirt out of the corner of his eye, tried to convince himself their dance didn't mean nothin' to her. But by the way she avoided his glance, he knew it had. And he made sure Jenny was in his arms for the last waltz.

He could do it, make a living and a life here. He could stake a claim, start a farm or help Jenny with her horse outfit. Still no way to know how that would go. He could boss a logging crew, swing an axe in the pure cold air of these mountains, haul the sixteen-footers to the river. He'd worked the jam crew before. He was good at it. And he could break up fights.

He paid his respects to Old Man Chivers and his younger, sickly wife. "Molly wouldn't let you use the hotel?"

Old Man Chivers spat through his beard. "Didn't ask. Womenfolk wanted a barn dance. Had to decorate it. Baubles and such. Hope it don't spook the horses. At least the rowdy ones stayed away. That helps maintain the calm."

"Don't see, um, Curtis. Or any of his group."

"We don't got no truck with them people." The old man snorted. "Tucker Creek people are trouble. Steve's from Ames Camp, the only one with decent folk far as I'm concerned. Only way we would've let Vi marry a logger."

Been a time when Pace would have been one of "them people." Drinkin', fightin', going down to the cribs. The trail had changed him, helped him, as he took care of all those other people and realized his responsibility. He couldn't go back. But he still didn't know which way was "forward."

He chatted with a few friends and caught up with Jenny as she packed up the hotel serving platters. She looked tired, shadows

126

under those blue eyes that were so different from Oona's, and he took the basket from her. "Come on. I'll walk you home."

Jenny looked up at him. "Why? I ain't a cripple."

"Why?" He fumbled. "Because it's what people do." When they go to a party together, he almost added.

But they hadn't been together, not really.

Jenny handed him her second basket. "Maybe we shouldn't worry so much about what people do and don't do." She put on her shawl, waved to Caroline, and preceded him out the door.

They walked in silence to the back door of the hotel.

She hesitated, gave him a quick peck on the cheek and, balancing her baskets, turned to go in.

It wasn't now or never — but it was now if he wanted to banish that vision in green from his mind and heart. "Jenny," he blurted. "Would you mind if I was to court you?"

He hadn't expected handsprings. He hadn't expected her question, either.

"Why?"

"Why — because. We get on well, and we can help each other out. I can work the horse farm with you. Be stronger together.

We're together all the time anyway."

"Yeah. Yeah, we are." Jenny nodded, her face thoughtful. "What about the trail?"

"I won't go back." And as he said it, he knew it was true. Might not stay in Hall's Mill, but his days hauling strangers were done.

Jenny considered that. Her lovely face, tipped up to his, was pale in the moonlight. She was considering his proposal. No sense dancing around it. That's what his question to her really was.

"Like you said, we're together all the time anyway — supper, ridin'," she pointed out in that practical way of hers. "Wouldn't be much different."

"Except we'd be workin' toward a marriage," he said, equally reasonable.

Jenny's eyes, wide in the silver light, took his measure.

An owl hooted somewhere, followed by a tired argument from the saloon.

He held his breath. He had never proposed to anyone before.

"Pace. That ain't what you want, and you know it."

If he had proposed before, maybe he would have been ready for her rejection, which was said in a calm, reproving way with a hint of a smile on her full red lips.

Oh, Jenny knew him too well.

"I — I —"

"Stop gaping." She gave him a gentle shove. "She ain't left yet. Go talk to her."

"Will you — ?"

"I'll be fine. Now go!"

He broke into a run, past the groups of two and three walking slowly toward their cabins, past a father with a sleeping child against his shoulder, past Steve's logger friends mounting up for the dark ride back to camp. To where Oona was leaving the barn, her head down as she walked across the square, the green gown shimmering in the light that still spilled from the building.

She looked up at his footsteps and her beautiful face was stripped of anything but longing for — for what?

Him?

She couldn't want him. Not Oona. Not Pace. Not him.

They stared at each other as the square emptied around them. "Did you — did you want something?" she finally asked in a small voice, an un-Oona-like voice.

His breath came short and rapid then barely at all. "Did you — do you — can I walk you home?"

"I shall — I shall be disappointed if you don't. And delighted if you do."

He picked her up by the waist and swung her, there in the darkened square until she threw back her head in laughter. Then he kissed her. Hard.

Pace had come back. Back to claim her.

Oh, he had felt it, too, in the dance and before and after, the energy between them that had a life of its own. Oona waited, she had all the time in the world, until he picked her up and swung her and kissed her, right there in the darkened street. His lips were firm and soft at the same time, and she kissed him back hungrily.

He drew her into the shadows around the barn. "I love you." His voice was hoarse. "I never said that before, not to no one, not to any living being. You know? This is what I want. You and me."

Oh, how she knew.

"I love you, Pace." The words she had never said to anyone but Kevin and that, as a child. They were so different. And she had Ireland. Could they make a life, a world of their own? Pace Williams loved her, Oona Moriarty. And as he claimed her lips again, she realized that this tough mountain man was trembling. But so was she.

He touched her hair, gave her a trembling smile. "It's late. But we need to talk."

"We will talk. Tomorrow, and the next day, and the next." She pressed her lips to his again, briefly, and once again relished the feeling of his strong arms around her.

There was only one Pace Williams. And he wanted her.

Pace lay awake on his pallet. The one-room shack was as black as the night outside, the quiet night with all the revelers gone home. But he didn't need light to think of "her." Bernadette had always brought her own glow. Was it strange, was it disloyal to think of another woman on, well, the happiest night of his life? No. Whatever was good about him, he'd learned from Bernadette. Whatever it was that made Oona love him, he'd learned from Bernadette.

She had been seventeen, the oldest girl in Our Lady's Home. She had long since graduated eighth grade, as high as the orphanage school went, and she'd never been adopted. Pace had thought a family would be crazy not to want her. But they hadn't, and there were few jobs for decent women. So she'd stayed on at the home, cooking and managing the kitchen to earn her keep. There was talk that the nuns had offered to teach her so she could join them. Be a shame, Pace had thought, to put all that blooming beauty under a veil.

"She" had been a beautiful girl, dark hair like Oona but shorter, with the same white skin and blue eyes, a face that shone above the drab dresses and aprons the nuns provided. But it was her kindness that had drawn him. She had a way of making him feel like the only kid in the room. Not a bad feeling for an orphan.

He'd had a crush on her, who wouldn't, and volunteered to help with the dishes most every night, along with two other smitten sixth-graders.

Bernadette sang as they worked. She always thanked the boys, and after cleanup, there was usually some treat, a cup of cocoa in the winter, a game of checkers, a quick concoction of bread, butter, and sugar for her boys.

And the dance lessons for two weeks in April, three boys taking turns stumbling around her in the cavernous convent kitchen, Bernadette's soft laugh as she coached them. "Alvin, put your hand on my waist. I don't bite." "Charlie, you're the man, you have to lead. One, two, three." And her joyous laughter when Pace had gotten brave and swung her.

As he had done with Oona.

Bernadette. If it hadn't been for her none

of this would have happened — the running, the trail, Oregon Country. Michael, Caroline, Jenny. She'd shaped his life, more than any beliefs he held, more than his own parents. Would it have been better if they'd never met? Never.

Because then there would have been no Oona.

13

Sunday dinner at the Hall's Mill Inn didn't amount to much more than the daily meals — a second biscuit with the stew, maybe a second choice of pie. But it was good enough for the bachelor loggers who wandered in from the woods, who were tired of beans.

And it was good enough for Pace.

He sat alone at his corner table, stayed to himself except for one glare from Victor Curtis, but it didn't bother him none. More time to think about Oona, the green dress, the kisses. And the promise in those kisses. How his world had changed, in less than twenty-four hours. Pace wiped his mouth on his sleeve and pushed his bowl away. "Molly, you done it again," he said.

As she cleared dishes from the other end of the plank table, Molly Davis gave him a fleeting smile. "Ain't much. Many hands make light work. You and Jenny ridin' to-day?"

"Nope. She's spendin' the afternoon with Sadie. Readin' to her, maybe taking a walk."

"She's good with her," Molly said.

Jenny was about as good with the little mute girl as anybody, which wasn't saying much. And he doubted if they'd have ridden anyway. Not today. Not when he had to talk to Oona. He'd seen her only briefly, when she'd poked her head out of the kitchen to remind Jenny of something and spotted him at the far table. But she'd smiled and their eyes had held with the memory of last night. Yes, they'd talk.

"You can take Rebel out if you want." Jenny had flung the words over her shoulder as she disappeared with a tray of dishes.

He was still the only person she trusted with Rebel. He just might do that. He had some thinkin' to do. Nothing wrong with riding alone, especially on Rebel. Or maybe he'd take a nap. It was Sunday. Nobody could stop him. Then he'd call on Oona. And think about Oona. On Rebel.

He was skirting the side of the hotel when he heard a clear voice, a decidedly feminine voice, lifted in song. The words were some ancient language, the tone plaintive and sad. His heart began to pound. Who else could it be? He followed the sound to the back porch and the uncovered wood platform where Molly received deliveries or beat rugs.

And where Oona sat on a stool and dried her long black hair in the sunlight. It fell almost to her waist, glistening like licorice candy as she combed it strand by strand and sang. She wore a faded blue dress, but she wore it like a queen. A queen with bare feet peeking out from under her skirt.

As he hesitated in the shadows, she waved him over.

"Don't be shy, Pace. I am modest, but I had five brothers."

Pace couldn't have walked away if he'd wanted to. This was his woman now. He paused to let that sink in before he sat on an overturned packing crate. "That was real pretty. Maybe the prettiest thing I ever heard."

Oona, no longer "Miss Oona," laughed softly. " 'Tis Gaelic. The words aren't so pretty. It is the ballad of Deirdre of the Sorrows, one of the great, tragic Irish queens."

"What'd she do?" He stretched out his legs, cocked his head in her direction, and tried not to look at those feet. Long . . . slender . . . perfect. If things worked out, he'd have the rest of his life to look at them.

Oona's voice took on a singsong quality,

the storytelling voice he'd heard in Mike. "Deirdre was the most beautiful woman in Ireland. But a druid prophesied that she was marked for death and the ruin of the land. King Conchobar wanted her for himself, and he kidnapped her when she was still a child and kept her in isolation until she was old enough to marry. But she fell in love with a young warrior, Naoise, and they fled to Scotland with his brothers. They had a daughter and were blissfully happy."

"I'm guessin' they didn't stay that way." In his experience, nobody ever did.

"No." Oona's smile held its own sorrows. "Wherever they went, the king in that area wanted her and threatened Naoise and his brothers. So they finally returned to Ireland, on Conchobar's promise of safety. But he had Naoise and his brothers killed. He forced Deirdre to marry him.

"But she loathed Conchobar and made no secret of it, so to punish her, he gave her in marriage to Eogan mac Durthacht, the very man who had killed her husband and brothers. As she was being taken to Eogan, Conchobar taunted her, and she threw herself from the chariot, dashing her head on the rocks."

Pace swallowed. These Irish, they didn't

soften the blows. "Hope that never happens to you."

Oona tossed her head, and the sun turned the drops of water to diamonds. "I was hoping I'd see you. After last night."

"Yeah. That was — somethin'. When did you know?"

"I've been thinkin' about you, and trying not to, since the day I dunked you. And I couldn't stop thinking about you after the night with the guns. Faith, and I love you, Pace."

He had never expected to hear those words, not here or anywhere else, and certainly not from her. He stood up, pulled Oona to her feet and into his arms, and lowered his lips to hers in the spring sunshine. When it was over, she rested against his shoulder, where she fit real well. "I love you too," he whispered.

She looked up at him. "What will you tell Jenny?"

"Jenny don't love me. Not that way. We were both alone. We got on well. We had nothing better to do." He searched for words. Hard to do with her so close. "It was . . . safe."

But nothing with Oona Moriarty would ever be safe.

"Besides, it was her idea, me comin' back

for you," he added.

The corners of Oona's lips turned up. "Remind me to thank her."

He was at home with this woman. All the years of wandering, all the years of looking for her in every woman he met, though he hadn't realized it until now. Finally home. "I can get a claim, build us a house. If I start clearing trees now, we'd be in it by fall. That gives you some time to — to do what women do. To get ready for marriage." He held his breath. This was where this was goin', wasn't it?

She drew back a little, grasped his forearms, and her dark blue eyes gleamed with challenge. "Come with me first, Pace. To Ireland."

"Whoa. Wait a minute . . ."

Well, one didn't change a Moriarty by telling them one loved them.

"You're an experienced gunman, a good horseman, a leader. You could make a difference. We'll take down the landlord who had Kevin killed. That will send them a message. Then we'll take down another one, until they get the point. 'Til England lets go. Not Hawthorne, that's too much of a risk, but there are others."

He disengaged himself a little, though it hurt to let her go. "I can't do it."

"Why?"

"You should let it go. Build a life here. You can't change nothin' over there. Don't borrow trouble." He had spent a lifetime not borrowing trouble, and it had found him anyways.

She wouldn't whine, but she would stand her ground. That was Oona. His Oona, now. "What did you think we'd do?"

Pace shrugged. "Start a farm like everyone else or some other work. Make a life here."

She shook her head, the water droplets scattering in the sunlight. "Not 'til I'm done with Ireland. I thought you'd go with me. They took everything, Pace. If it wasn't for them, I'd be married now with a child or two. A full life, not a spinster shopkeeper. Three years in a convent. I don't even know if he would have waited. I'll never know, now." She must have seen something change in his face, and she hung on tightly. "I'm sorry. I did not mean it that way. But don't you see, Pace? I would have had a life."

He was offering her a life. He looked down at her, down into those pleading eyes, and dropped his hands to his sides. "You want to do this because of Kevin. You want me to get revenge for your fiancé."

" 'Tisn't just that. I want to find Tom. I want to find Caitrin and the babies. I worry about them." She stretched out her hands.

But she could do those things without a posse. And Mike was already planning to find and help Tom, to bring him here, out of danger. Did they need Oona to help search, too? Did they?

Pace backed away. "I got to think," he said. "I just — I got to think." He almost ran from the hotel, saddled Rebel, and rode into the woods. The sun turned the leaves of the hardwoods a brighter green, made dappled patterns on the forest floor. But the wind was up, and storm clouds gathered in the distance. Pace pushed Rebel as hard as he dared.

Some of Pace's worst nights had been the ones when Roy came. Roy would slam into the orphanage kitchen without knocking. He'd haul Bernadette up from her chair or grab her by the waist with both hands and kiss her hard.

Bernadette hadn't seemed to like that much. She got out of his arms as soon as she could. Sometimes she'd mumbled a feeble, "Roy, what will the children think?"

And Roy would sweep a chilling glance over the three silent boys. "Don't matter what they think."

Roy was a big man even to a tall eleven-year-old. Pace had seen him split a board with his hand once, down at the square, just showing off. He was a stonemason, building fireplaces and chimneys, and his muscles rippled under his plaid shirts. He wasn't handsome, had a scar running down his cheek, but nobody mentioned it. Nobody dared. Last person who made fun of Roy now walked with a cane. Best to leave him alone.

Roy was supposed to be courtin' Bernadette. He'd asked the sisters, formal and all, because she didn't have a pa, and they'd said yes. He'd been so polite. The nuns didn't know what he was really like.

Bernadette went off with him twice a week.

Pace didn't know where they went — but he'd sneaked out of bed those nights, slipped down the back staircase and watched from the pantry until she came home. Sometimes, she came back with a bruise on her cheek. Sometimes, she came back crying. Sometimes, she found him and scolded him gently. Sometimes, she didn't.

And one night she came back cradling her right arm in her left. She hung her shawl on a peg, dumped tealeaves in a cup, and poured water from the kettle on the back burner. But the tea sat forgotten as she put her head in her hands, and her shoulders heaved with sobs.

That'd been enough for Pace. He'd crept from his hidey-hole and put a tentative hand on her shoulder.

She had turned to him, tears sparkling in her beautiful eyes. "You should not be up. You'll be tired in school tomorrow."

He didn't care, and he knew she knew he didn't care. "Don't matter." He'd pulled out the chair next to her. "Why do you let 'im do it?"

Bernadette had cradled her arm. "He doesn't mean it. He's like a lot of men. Gets a few drinks in him and he loses control. It doesn't — mean anything."

Even at eleven, Pace had known it meant something. "What did you do this time?"

Bernadette's voice went flat like the linens she ironed. "I laughed at someone else's joke at the party."

Pace had felt like hitting something himself, but not her. Never her. "That ain't so bad," he remembered saying. "It ain't worth this."

"You're right. It isn't." He knew she was upset because she didn't correct his grammar.

He scraped his chair closer, whispered furiously lest someone come downstairs and find them. "Do you hafta marry him?"

Bernadette smiled without an ounce of humor. "What else can I do? There aren't many jobs for women in this town, and I haven't the money to get anywhere else."

"What about — here?" He hated to see all this beauty and joy smothered under a black habit. But even the convent would be better than a life of Roy — and Pace would still see her.

Bernadette shook her head. "The sisters asked me more than once. But I don't have a vocation. I want children, a home of my own." She hadn't added, "And a husband."

"Do the sisters know what he does to you?"

"No, and you will not tell them."

Pace smashed one fist into another and didn't even mark the pain. He had to help her. He was a strong boy, nigh on to a man, and his changing voice barely croaked as he laid out his proposition.

"You an' me, we'll run away." He looked at her steadily. "I can do a man's work. I'm almost twelve, an' I don't want to be here either. We'll go somewhere, get a room. I'll work and you can keep house. You can be my ma."

She looked at him with eyes that were sad, knowing, and loving. "You are a fine boy.

And you have a future. I can't tie you down that way. Roy and I will be — all right." She'd pushed back an errant lock of his hair. "Go to bed, now. Running away never fixed anything."

A world and a lifetime away, Pace kicked Rebel's side and urged him to go faster, giving him his head in an open field. No. Running didn't fix anything. But he'd since learned that neither did staying.

Hall's Mill, where he'd pondered settling, would be nothing now without Oona at his side. Worse than nothing. Every place they'd walked or talked would become a mockery to him. What a difference a day made.

He could do it again, take to the trail, shrug off Hall's Mill and the memory of the Irishwoman, lose himself in the work of caring for strangers. He'd run away before; he could do it again.

But would there ever be anything to run to?

With shaking fingers, Oona braided her hair. That was that. He wouldn't go with her. No, she wasn't just seeking justice for Kevin. She had planned this long before she'd learned he was dead, in those lonely nights in her room in the Dublin convent. Through Matins, Lauds, floor-scrubbing, and silent meals. She missed Kevin, yes, but in truth she didn't know who or what he'd be today. He had carried her books, shown off for her in the schoolyard. Had he lived, would their love have survived? Based on what she'd said and felt today, most likely not. She loved Pace as a woman grown, not as a girl with a dream. But Kevin hadn't deserved to die the way he did. And she would always carry her family with her, the ones who'd died, the ones who were missing, the ones who were somewhere living a life far worse than they deserved.

She had killed the landlord's son and set in motion this unthinkable chain of events. What else could she have done? Given in to him? Never. Talked up a storm and teased him out of it? Doubtful. But there had to have been a way besides killing. Hadn't there? Oona drew a deep shuddering breath. She *would* see this through. Pace or no Pace, Michael or no Michael.

Because it had all been her fault.

14

"You're here late." Mike's voice broke the hush of the livery stable at night.

Pace swung around at the sound. "Yeah, I did a quick run after supper. Ames Camp. I'm gonna take care of Rebel and head on to bed."

Didn't Mike have something to do? He worked here, after all. Maybe they could avoid this conversation, the one Pace had been dodging for a week.

But Mike settled in, his tall form propped against the doorframe, his flannel-clad arms crossed. Mike, with all the time in the world. "So. You and Oona?"

Pace's skin warmed. He hadn't blushed since — well, never. "Yeah." He hung Rebel's saddle on a hook and patted the horse's rump. "Good boy. You done real good today."

He wiped the horse down in slow, sure strokes. Longer it took, less time he had to

147

look at Mike. Was Mike mad? Did he think Pace wasn't good enough for his sister? Well, Pace wouldn't argue that. If anyone knew Pace, the good and the bad, it was Mike Moriarty. Working a wagon train did that to people.

No. Mike didn't know him. Not really.

Mike crossed his arms tighter. Pace knew that stance. Mike was settling in for a quick round of stubbornness. Of course, he'd want to protect his sister. And he knew the man Pace had been, at least during their time together. Pace hadn't been above a drink, a brawl, or buying the company of a pretty woman. Jenny was a living reminder of who he'd been.

"Oona's a good girl," Mike was saying.

Pace rubbed a little harder. "I ain't planning to take advantage of her if that's what you're meanin'. I aim to do this right." Her face came to him as it often did, those blue eyes that could spark with mischief — or anger.

She was worth waiting for. He just didn't know how long he'd have to wait. "I would be good to her," he ground out. "I wouldn't hurt her."

Mike shifted a little. " 'Tis not what I meant."

"What, then? It's late. Ain't got time for

148

riddles."

It was late; the respectable people were in bed. Ed Petersen had shooed out his last bar customers. An owl hooted somewhere from the woods.

"Oona, she's a handful." Mike didn't miss much.

"Yeah, I figured that out," Pace said. "Before I even met her."

"You know she's goin' back to the old country."

"Yeah, I know." Probably knew more about it than Mike did. Had Mike seen Oona's gun collection? "Tried to talk her out of it."

"Try again." There was grimness in Mike's voice. Pace had heard it before but only when Mike talked about Ireland.

"Won't do no good."

"You have to try. Because if Oona makes it back to Ireland, she'll never leave again."

"She told me —" She'd said she'd come back. Promised him. And he'd hung on to it like a drowning man. Oona wouldn't lie to him.

Mike waited a heartbeat. "I mean she'll never leave Ireland alive."

It was the answer Pace had dreaded, had talked himself out of countless times. Oona was smart. She was brave. She would get the job done.

"They will kill her," Mike said. "String her from a tree, most likely. Kevin O'Halloran was smart and tough. He was the best shot in our village, and he couldn't outwit them. What do you think they'd do to a woman?"

Pace stopped the rubdown. He bent his head. Could Mike see him struggling for air? Hearing it from Mike sharpened the truth and put it into unwelcome focus. Pace could tell himself she'd be fine, she'd return to him in triumph, joking about the ordeal, telling the stories with that Moriarty flair. But Mike knew what she'd face when she stepped off that boat.

Mike pressed on. "If she's caught as part of the underground — and she will be — she'll be hanged. Made an example of. The English won't care that she's young and comely. They won't care that she's a woman. Faith, and they'll enjoy it all the more. 'Tis why Tom and I put her in the convent in the first place."

Pace looked up at last. Mike's arms were still folded, his chin thrust out. A pose Pace had seen dozens of times over the past two years, Mike Moriarty digging in his heels. Why should Oona be any less stubborn? And would he love her as much if she were?

150

Mike's voice gentled. "You don't know what it's like over there. You've always had this." Mike waved one of his arms, to encompass not only the livery stable but the town, Oregon Country, and the continent. "America. The chance to be someone. To be free."

Free? Pace choked back a laugh. If Mike only knew.

"You should go with her," he flung back. "You know these people, what to do, what not to do. Better'n I would."

Would he feel better if Mike went back with Oona? Not really, he'd lose both of them. But it was better than her going alone.

"I can't go. They'd arrest me the minute I stepped on solid ground. And I've got Caroline. I wouldn't put her in harm's way. Especially now."

Oh. Yeah. That. A child on the way. One more thing Pace would most likely not have with Oona. He twisted the water out of the cloth, hung the cloth on a peg and began to brush Rebel. "I'll talk to her." And though Mike was in charge here he added, "Get out, now. Go on home."

Pace walked back through town, what there was of it, and stopped in front of the hotel. A single lamp gleamed inside the wide front window. There she was, setting the tables for breakfast. She still helped Molly out, besides running the store, and he had to admire her ambition. Along with everything else.

And her grace as she moved among the splintered tables and placed each fork just so. He couldn't see her face, at first — just that straight back and the fall of hair, released from the braid and barely restrained by a ribbon. She turned, and he could see a faint smile. He imagined her humming. What would it be like to come home to this woman? She deserved her own kitchen, her own fireside. He'd been willing to give it to her. But it wasn't enough.

Why, of all the women in the world, did he have to love this one? He raised a hand to knock on the window.

But she saw him first, and her face lit up. "Pace," she mouthed. He climbed the rickety steps but she was already at the door, throwing it open to be framed by the light. "What brings you here this late?"

"I just —" There was no right answer. "I wanted to see ya."

"Then see me you shall." Oona pulled him inside. "Let's sit for a few minutes. We didn't talk much at supper."

Yeah, sometimes they didn't, just sat like

an old married couple. But if he didn't act soon, they wouldn't get a chance to be a young married couple.

They sat on a bench. He kneaded her hands between his. Soft hands, despite the work they'd always done, but strong. "You work too hard."

Oona shrugged. "I need the money. And there's nothing else to do in this town."

'Course not. There wasn't even a government to overthrow.

"Oona, I don't want you to go back to Ireland. I got a bad feeling about it." He cleared his throat. "Not just about Kevin, I could live with that, but the whole business. Ain't safe for a man, let alone you. I really — I wish you'd stay."

"You've talked to Michael."

Oh, she was sharp.

"Yeah, we talked. But I didn't need no convincin'. It's nasty business over there, and I don't want to lose you."

She looked down at their twined hands. "Pace, if I don't go back, don't do something, I'll be dishonoring my family. My mother — she would have loved you. My brother, Tomeen, and the little ones. Turned out of their home. Why should I survive? What gave me the right?"

Was it really about Kevin? Or even her folks?

"You feel guilty." The three words echoed around the shadowed room.

"If I hadn't smiled at the landlord's son, if I'd worn something different that day —"

"No." He stood up and pulled her with him, looked into the beautiful haunted face. "Wasn't your fault no more than Harry Bennett was your fault. It's — it's the way things are over there. Were. You don't have to put up with that any more. You can stay here, marry me. I'll keep you safe."

She hesitated a second too long. "Me? In this place?"

"I got some money. Don't have to be Oregon Country. We'll go anywhere you want. Exceptin' Ireland."

Her blue eyes were dark but luminous in the dimly-lit room. She kissed him lightly. "Then I'll come back. For Ireland's the place I need to be right now."

She tipped her face up to his, and he kissed her again, hard. Relished the feel of her lips on his, the feel of her in his arms. And released her before he relished it too much. No woman had ever stirred him like this. And he'd never wanted to keep a woman pure as he did this one. Until the right time. Let it be soon.

He didn't know who to address. Certainly not God. He released the plea to anyone or anything that could answer it. He'd never known he was lonely until he'd had someone to miss.

He touched a gleaming strand of her hair. "I'll be leavin' now." He'd better. "Will I see you tomorrow?"

"I'll be at the store all day. And I'll bring you supper."

It was all he had, at least for now. It was more than he'd ever had. But it would never be enough.

Guilt. He pushed open the door of his cabin, kicked off his boots, and sprawled on his pallet. Well, he could tell her a thing or two about guilt. Should he tell her? The guilt of someone who should never have been born?

No. Not yet.

Because it would hurt her to hear it even more than it would hurt him to tell it.

15

If only Joe Foster would stop talking. Usually the garrulous man took too much of
Oona's time, causing people behind him in
line to fidget and fume. Today, there was no
line, but she couldn't wait for him to leave.

"Ain't natural," Foster said, and spit out a
plug of tobacco to the packed-earth floor.
"They should have their own school. Iffen
they need school at all."

As she counted out his ten penny nails,
Oona clung to her composure. "I would
think anyone who makes the trip out here
deserves a chance." She should know. She'd
done it virtually alone, and for what?

"Coloreds need to know their place. And
it ain't in a white school." Foster looked
around the empty store as if waiting for ap-
plause. When it didn't come, he counted
out his pennies from a ragged canvas sack.

Oona tucked Foster's money in the cash
box and wondered how much more of him

she could take. "How is the house coming?"

"Goin' out there today," Foster answered in his liquid drawl. "Cain't get much done in the snow, but I can work on the inside. How's your brother's comin' along?"

"Well enough. He and Mr. Williams worked out there this past Saturday."

Joe Foster drew himself up and made the proclamation he made every time he asked and she answered. "It don't get done by lookin' at it. Cabins don't build theirselves." He added, "I may be back for more nails dependin' on how it goes."

She hoped it went well.

It wasn't fair, not fair at all, that the Jackson family had to put up with this after crossing the country alone. No wagon train would take them on, Michael had told her. Two adults and two children fighting the desert, the river crossings, the mountains — and now this. She could only hope what they'd left behind was worse. For Mrs. Jackson, a former slave, it must have been.

Oona needed air. She pushed open the door and leaned against the outside of the mercantile. A bright day, the sun glinting off a late snowfall, most likely the last. Would Pace stop by? He often slipped in during his courier runs, sometimes making a purchase, sometimes not even pretending

157

to need anything but her. She needed him, too, like light and air. But did she need him enough?

Oona blinked in the sunlight. Surely, that couldn't be Caroline, leading a flock of children across the square like a mother duck with her ducklings. Caroline, clad in bonnet and shawl, an early spring breeze teasing the strings of the bonnet. Caroline's back straight, as if someone had stuffed a poker in it.

Fewer than ten children trailed behind her. The three Dale girls with the middle one, Rowena, running ahead. She already had a nickname in town, "Rambunctious Rowena." Two pale, silent boys who came in from the hills every day, riding pillion on an old swaybacked nag. And the two Jackson children.

Caroline's jaw was set, an attitude Oona had never seen in her sister-in-law, not that she'd looked all that much.

The children looked terrified, except for Rowena, who reached her first. "Miz Davis said we couldn't use the hotel any more for class on account of we have school with the coloreds," she said, seemingly in a single breath. "An' the mothers pulled their children out, 'cept for our Mama. She says so long as we get us an education, she doesn't

158

care who's on the next bench or who we have to share a reader with. And Mrs. Moriarty told Miz Davis —"

"Hush, Rowena." Caroline made a gesture, and the little girl subsided into sputtering.

Oona tried to sort it out. "What is she telling me, then, Caroline?"

Caroline brushed at a strand of hair escaped from the bonnet. Oona had never seen her anything but immaculate. "Mrs. Davis told us we couldn't hold class in the hotel any longer. Parents were complaining about — about —"

"About the coloreds," Rowena put in helpfully.

"Rowena, you hush and let Mrs. Moriarty talk." Elora, Rowena's older sister, moved to put an arm around Deborah Jackson.

Oona knew the Jackson children by sight, their dusky faces standing out as their mother hurried them through town or they waited while she conducted her meager transactions at the store. The boy, Elijah, twelve or a tall ten, barefoot and in overalls like the other town boys. The little girl, Deborah, seven or eight, in a dress with tucks and ruffles, stitched from remnants, Oona could tell, but stitched with love and skill. Mrs. Jackson had been the head seamstress on a plantation, according to Caroline, until Moses bought and married her.

"So I told her we'd be moving out. The only other public building is the saloon and we can't go there. So we were hoping —" Caroline looked up at Oona, her hazel eyes wide.

Oona could see why Michael couldn't resist this woman. Faith, and it must be even harder for a man. "You could meet in the back storeroom, set up a couple of benches. For now. I'd have to ask Annie —"

"Annie Two Stars is a mixed-breed," Caroline said. "She won't object."

"Well, then." Oona drew a deep breath. What was she getting herself into? "Go and get your slates and such, and I'll see about making room." Oona propped the door open.

The mercantile wasn't much of a store, but then Hall's Mill wasn't much of a town. The frame walls gave the impression that a child could tip them over with one push. Seemed like the merchandise held the building up: crates of bullets and guns, piles of fabric, barrels of dried beans and corn-meal, saddles and bridles, axes, and hoes. Everything Annie Two Stars could sell to a person carving a life out of the Oregon woods.

160

And now a school. But really, what choice did Oona have?

"Don't seem as if you had much choice." Pace swirled a chunk of bread in the juice of his beans.

"Faith, and I didn't." Oona relaxed on her overturned barrel. These suppers were sweet, after both of their workdays, when they could convene by Pace's fire and share their stories.

Pace's cabin wasn't much, even smaller and damper than her brother's place. His bed was a pallet on the canvas-covered floor, his other furniture barrels and crates. None of the shacks had chimneys, and the smoky fire drifted out a hole in the wall. But at the end of a work day, there was no place she'd rather be.

Sweet. As long as they didn't let it get too sweet. There were few enough chaperones in this Oregon Country, and Pace's kisses awakened feelings she hadn't known she had. Feelings far more powerful than she'd had even for Kevin.

"The school board, those men who appointed themselves and had money set aside to pay her, came in at the end of the day, and I'm thinking they told her that her services are no longer required. So she's teaching in the store. Without a salary." She paused to remember the three men showing up at the mercantile, Caroline's calm invitation to discuss things in the back room. Three men leaving after an hour, Caroline spending another hour alone before she emerged with reddened eyes. Whatever they'd said to Caroline, she hadn't liked it. But it hadn't broken her. Oona's sweet little sister-in-law had a spine.

"It shouldn't be too difficult," Oona went on. "With only seven children, she can get through the school day in half the time. Better for Caroline in case she's feeling — poorly." She blushed and hurried on. Pregnancy wasn't an acceptable topic even with one's fiancé. "And I'll be grateful for the company," Oona concluded. "It gets slow in the mornings."

Pace forked another scoop of beans. "You got any problem with coloreds?"

Like a fist to her stomach, the words brought back the bowing and scraping, the lowered eyes when the landlord's family passed by. The little humiliations they'd all taken for granted. And the unvarnished fact that because of their race and religion, they would always be servants in their own country. "I do not," she said. "Not after Ireland."

Pace drained the coffee in his tin cup. "I got no problem either. Not after runnin' the wagon train and seeing what folks can do to one another. White folks, brown folks, colored folks. It don't matter."

She'd hoped he would say something like that, and she beamed her approval across his damp shack. He was a good man. "Thank you, Pace."

"Ain't a good way to live, setting one group of people above another," he went on, the firelight highlighting the planes in his face. "Ain't fair."

What had he seen? What had he been? Pace had secrets. She'd known from the start that he wasn't telling her everything. An "everything" that could make them stronger, or shatter what they had into pieces. Should she tell him about Maeve? No, that would bring on the brooding look that overtook him whenever she spoke of Kevin. "It was like that at home," she said instead. "We weren't judged by our skin, but we were by everything else."

And yet here she was, goin' back.

The unspoken question dangled between them, as it always did. A fool's journey. A journey that would more'n likely get her killed.

A journey she felt she had to make, for a people as beaten down as the coloreds were here. For her parents, for the lost Caitrin, for Mike, and his years of wandering. For Kevin.

Pace could go with her. Wasn't as if he had anything better to do, or any better place to do it. But it was someone else's fight, and he'd gotten too good at keepin' his head down. Wasn't no one better at it. What did he have to offer her? A leaky shack and a man with more of a past than anyone needed.

He could take himself a claim, build a log cabin. Mike would help. Pace had spent enough Saturdays helping Mike. He couldn't protect the coloreds. Nobody could, but he could protect Oona, their land, their house, and their children running free. Safe at last.

But was that even what she wanted?

Three days later, Oona pushed open the door to the mercantile and smiled when she heard humming in the back. No matter how early Oona got to the store Caroline was there before her, letting herself in with the spare key, straightening benches or organizing supplies. To Oona, it seemed that she was determined to make this work, to show

Hall's Mill that they couldn't break her. Oona had to admit it showed some courage.

Just as she had to admit most of Hall's Mill didn't like it. They couldn't boycott the mercantile, there were no other stores within fifty miles, but they made their opinions known with pinched lips, rolled eyes, and murmured asides.

Oona counted their change, bagged their purchases, helped them find things and raged inside. Had she come all this way, three thousand miles and then some, to find a people who thought the same as the landlords? What had been the point of it all?

No. Pace wasn't like that, nor her brother. Nor his Caroline, who held class every day for no wages for seven children in the storeroom of a mercantile. But were they enough?

Caroline came out shortly after noon, exhausted but smiling, leaning her arms on the counter, her hazel eyes aglow in her small face.

"You've had a good day, then?" Oona asked.

"I did, indeed. That Elora Dale — she can read anything! She's reading on an adult level. I'm loaning her books from my own collection. She's outpaced the reading primer. And Elijah Jackson has caught up to his grade in mathematics."

"Who was teaching the Jacksons before?"

"Their father. Moses was — is — a free man, and the Quakers taught him back in Massachusetts."

Mayhap this country wasn't all bad. But faith, and it was exhausting to ferret out the good.

"Will you be headin' out now?" Oona asked.

Caroline dimpled, the sweet smile that always made Oona see what had drawn Michael to her. "In a few minutes. Could you set aside a half cup of sugar? Jenny brought me some berries she picked. She called them huckleberries, and I'm planning to make a pie. Would you and Pace like to come over later?"

Oona and Pace. How quickly they'd become a couple in the eyes of this community. And how little that community really knew. "Sure, and we will," she said. "But the sugar is getting low. I'm hopin' the freighters can get through the passes soon."

With a swish of skirts, Caroline headed back to the storeroom.

Oona bent over her ledger. A strangled cry brought her head up. "Caroline?"

Was Michael's wife ill? Was the baby coming too soon? Or had Victor Curtis acted on one of his veiled suggestions?

Oona dropped the ledger and ran to the storeroom.

No, Caroline was alone, standing and staring at the back door, at a sign scrawled in charcoal on a flimsy piece of wood, and dangling by a bent nail. In clumsy block letters, it voiced an ugly word used against coloreds, one that sickened Oona.

Caroline had gone white, too white, but her back was erect and her voice controlled. "Oona, please get Michael."

"Who could have done it?" Mike pounded one fist into another.

Pace shrugged. They'd been at this for an hour, huddled around the Moriartys' supper fire, trying to put a name and face to whoever hung the sign outside Caroline's schoolroom.

Caroline rested on the couple's pallet, a mug of steaming tea in one hand, a faded quilt tucked around her legs. She looked played-out, though Pace knew that could be deceptive. Despite her delicate looks, on the trail she'd proven herself as tough as they came. This involved kids, and Caroline was a mountain lion when it came to kids.

Mike was struggling to contain his fury and doing a poor job of it. Mike was a mountain lion when it came to Caroline.

And Oona was moving gracefully in someone else's kitchen, keeping their tin mugs full of tea, and starting the Moriartys' supper without being asked. Why shouldn't he look at her, imagine what could have been? Could still be, but a long shot, and growing longer every day.

"Jenny might know," Oona said. "She hears everything at that hotel. But she's knee-deep in supper right now."

"I'll ask her later." Mike frowned. "What about Mrs. Wilkins, Caroline? She never liked you back in Ohio."

"It was me she didn't like, Michael. Not an entire race of people." Pace marveled at the patience Caroline had with Mike. They were a good match in more ways than one. "And Mrs. Wilkins would have written 'No Negroes' on her best stationery." She took a sip of tea. "Besides, her husband is on the school board, and they already fired me."

"Joe Foster never liked the idea of Elijah and Deborah in the same school as the white children." Oona paused by the hearth. "He's said a few things at the store."

"And he's a leader here. The other men listen to him," Mike said, in the slow dawning way he accepted an idea that wasn't his own.

Pace knew that voice. "Foster ain't mean enough." Pace drained his tin mug.

"Maybe not to you. But Foster's a good place to start." Michael stretched until he could touch the shack's ceiling. "Come on then, Pace. If Mr. Foster didn't write this, he knows who did."

Pace didn't want no trouble. Never had. But he'd seen what Mike's temper could do. And if Roy found him here, or the even worse combination of Roy and Carl, he'd need Mike at his back. He uncoiled from the packing crate and followed his friend.

They found Joe Foster just in from working on his claim. With sleeves rolled up, Foster bathed his face and hands in a basin as his wife, Lucy, fried potatoes in the background, grease sizzling in the iron skillet. The odor of beans baked in molasses filled the two-room cabin.

Foster rubbed his face with a threadbare towel. "What can I do for you, Moriarty? Williams?" His voice held the twang of somewhere south of where Pace was raised. He was a hard worker, a family man, a pillar of what passed for a community here.

Pace leaned against the splintery door. He'd let Mike handle this one, at least until fists were needed.

Mike perched on an overturned crate without being invited. "You can tell me who wrote on the door of my wife's school. That should get us started."

"Wrote what?" Foster wrung out the towel in his strong hands. This man would do well in the West.

"Someone put a sign on the door that had a slur on it because she's teaching the Jackson children."

"Wasn't me." He remained casual and confident.

"How do I know that?" Pace had to admire Mike's patience. Maybe he was growin' up; maybe it was his religion.

Foster dropped the towel and looked directly at Mike for the first time. "Because I cain't write. Nor read."

It was a good argument but not good enough. "You could have put someone up to it," Mike said.

"Ain't no point in that. Miz Moriarty wants to mix coloreds and whites, up to her. Just not in a public school."

"So you don't want the Jacksons gone?"

"Long as they don't bother us, I don't care." Joe straddled the only real chair in the room. It was obviously his chair. The others would sit on packing crates and barrels pulled up to the makeshift table, but Joe reigned in this cabin. Joe's sleeves were rolled up to show powerful forearms, and a shadow of beard darkened his cheeks. "Look, Moriarty. My pa had a little farm in Georgia. Left it to my brother, which is why I'm out here. My pa didn't own slaves, but he didn't mix with coloreds either. It's the way the good Lord ordained it."

Pace didn't know enough about the Bible to argue that. But he liked Joe Foster well enough. Joe was a family man, a hard worker. Joe stayed to home at night, not setting foot in Petersen's bar. Would he lie?

Lucy Foster spoke from the hearth, where she ladled the beans and crispy fried potatoes on to tin plates. "We came here to get a better life, Mr. Moriarty. I can't read either. We want more for our young'uns. Our kids in school with coloreds — it's a step back for us. That's all. We don't mean no harm to them — or your missus."

Joe and Lucy's children came swarming in, and they clamored for a chance at the wash basin.

Joe walked Pace and Mike out, clapped a hand on Mike's shoulder. "Moriarty, you're a good man. But there's ways things is done, and it don't do no good to upset 'em."

"Do you have any idea —"

"Nobody in the village. Good night, Moriarty. Williams."

They walked away.

"Moriarty?"

They half-turned at Foster's call.

"I'd stay out of it if I were you."

They walked back to the Moriarty cabin, Mike ignoring the nods and waves of townspeople, some of them children who should have been in Caroline's school. Men like Joe Foster were coming home from working on their claims — the claims they'd risked the Oregon Trail to get to.

"Wasn't Foster," Pace said to Mike. "Mebbe a kid?"

The children with too much time on their hands.

"Maybe."

"You — you gonna tell her to back off? To stop teaching the coloreds?"

Mike lifted his head and stared at Pace. "That would mean they'd won, Pace. And I already saw that in Ireland." Mike opened the door to his cabin without a backward glance.

Out of habit, Pace ducked his head on the low doorway. There was Oona, his Oona Cathleen Moriarty, bent over the smoky fire, tasting something with a long spoon.

And Caroline seated at the table, two barrels with boards stretched between, with reading primers, pencils and slates spread across the surface. She looked up at Mike with a smile of defiance and love.

" 'T'would seem," Mike said, "that we have a fight on our hands."

16

Oona was late today, she'd stayed too long
at Pace's last night, and she picked up her
skirts and half-ran the last few feet to the
mercantile. The first of spring's freighters
had gotten through the mountains yesterday
with a load of precious commodities from
the East. But she stopped short as a voice,
rusty from tobacco and lack of use, called
to her.

"You get it all in?"

Annie Two Stars, the owner of the mercantile and nearly everything else in Hall's Mill,
halted her pony cart before the store. Too
big to walk or even ride, she got about in a
two-wheeled cart pulled by a matched team.
And get about Annie did, checking daily on
the store, the saloon, and the shacks she
rented to the dazed and desperate emigrants. Nobody knew where Annie had
come from or how she had gotten her
money. She was fluent in French and two

Indian dialects. In English, her fourth language, she read, wrote, and spoke on a child's level. But there was one language Annie had mastered: money.

"We got it all off the wagons and into the store. I'll be sorting and pricing this afternoon." Oona smiled at the big woman dressed in men's clothing, whose graying braids reached to her waist.

"Moses. He help."

Oona would be glad enough to see Moses Jackson, who'd unloaded the bulk of the new merchandise. If the job put a few more pennies toward the Jacksons' claim, so much the better.

Annie's leathered cheeks crinkled in a rare smile. "The school. Is good," she said before she lumbered toward the saloon to see — or harass — Ed Petersen.

Yes. The school, it was good. Oona had seen the Jackson children come alive, from both their new friends and Caroline's nurturing. The two boys from the hills still rode in together every day, and though they avoided adults, she heard them laughing and yelling at recess. And the Dale girls thrived, Elora, Ramona, and the invincible Rowena. And Deborah loved her friends.

Had Caroline's God made something good out of something very bad?

He'd never done that for Oona. Mayhap there were different gods. Hers sat in judgment, instilled fear. Eight years of parish school and three years in the convent hadn't changed her opinion. She couldn't say she didn't believe. But she was better off staying out of His way.

Oona made good use of her morning hours, unpacking crates of jarred vegetables, their colors rich behind the glass. A boon to both the bachelor loggers and the housewives who had arrived too late to put in gardens, who would reap their first western harvests next year. She wouldn't be here to see it.

She listened to the murmur from Caroline's improvised classroom, the occasional laughter. Caroline had found something she loved to do. Would Oona be that lucky? She'd never had a chance to ask herself what she wanted. She'd not really had a choice. She went to work in the manor house to help support the family, and then in the convent at eighteen.

The day was warmer and sunny, and it drew Oona outside at last. She propped the door open and swept the flat rock that served as a step. When she was done, she shaded her eyes and looked out over the settlement.

A group of urchins played in the middle of the baked mud street, some game of their own devising that seemed to involve their mothers' brooms and a small piece of wood. The objective appeared to be to swat the wood from one child to another, slipping it past the boys on the opposing team. They wore no uniforms, and only the boys themselves knew who their opposition was.

And Pace, who sat on his haunches coaching and cheering them on. He looked like a boy himself, although a rather large one, as a huge grin split his face and he yelled encouragement to both teams from the sidelines.

She had never seen him like this. He was always so serious, even with her. So controlled.

Two of the children called out to him to mediate a dispute. He unfolded his lean length and started toward them when he spotted her in the doorway. He shot her a quick grin — but their eyes held a moment too long.

She shut the mercantile door against the brightness of the day. Trembling, she leaned against the rough plank.

She loved him — loved his loyalty to Michael and Caroline, his generous spirit, the stories she'd heard of his courage on

177

the trail; loved the way he threw himself into playing with these children; loved the way he listened to her, his dark eyes fastened on her face, the quirk of a grin when she'd amused him; loved him for his kisses and his strong arms around her.

And she loved him in spite of his dark places, or perhaps, because of them. He seemed to have been hurt more deeply than she or anyone else would ever know, and she wanted to hold him in her arms until it didn't hurt any more.

She allowed herself to think of what it might be like if they were two different people. Having him come home to her at night, making a home for Pace, their children underfoot, their baby in his lap. Building something together.

But her dream put them in an Irish cottage, a thatched roof, and walls stained by centuries of peat fires. Not a western cabin.

If only Ma hadn't died by the roadside. If only Oona could lay her head on that broad lap and spill her story. *Oh, Ma, I'm in love again —*

Could one love two people at once? Did it matter, if one of them was dead?

It could never happen. Pace belonged to the West, and Oona belonged to Ireland. For better or worse.

She turned from the door and jumped when she saw Sadie, the mute girl from the hotel. "Sadie! I didn't know you were in here."

The girl's face did not change. It never did. Oona had never seen her smile. She was a mystery, as much as a mystery as whatever lay behind Pace's dark eyes.

Sadie handed Oona an empty crock with a brief note inside from Molly.

"Flour? Of course, I'll send some over." Oona moved to the bin and began to scoop. "What has she made that caused her to run out of flour? Cookies? Did Miss Jenny bake one of her wonderful pies?"

Sadie did not blink.

Oona sighed. Must be something she could do to help the child. She'd seen her hovering around Caroline's classroom back when it had been in the hotel. "Why don't you go to Mrs. Moriarty's school?" she pressed gently. "I know Miss Molly gives you some free time. It's a smaller group now, and you might enjoy it."

Sadie didn't answer. She never did. She took the crock of flour and left.

And as Oona held the door for Sadie, she looked for Pace. But the street was empty, the children scattered, and Pace was gone.

Moses Jackson arrived after dinner, after

the children had gone for the day, and Caroline had trudged home for the nap she now allowed herself. The usual smile wreathed Moses's round face.

Oona didn't know what the man had to smile about.

He pried crates open with a narrow metal bar and lifted out the heavier items, plow handles and pitchforks, wheels for a buckboard, and set them on the earthen floor. He sang as he worked, haunting minor-key tunes about Israel's oppression in Egypt, about chariots coming for the faithful, and the glimpse of a Heaven he would most likely never see on earth. His rich voice rolled out the mournful lyrics.

"When Israel was in Egypt's land (let my people go) Oppressed so hard she could not stand (let my people go) Go down Moses, way down in Egypt land. Tell old Pharaoh to let my people go."

Oona could no longer keep silent. "That's a beautiful song," she said.

Moses's teeth flashed in his dark face. "Thanks, Miss Oona. It be how I got my name. My full name is Go Down Moses Jackson."

"How did you learn the songs?"

"They be spirituals. The songs of my people. They sing them when they're workin' the fields."

"Did Dulcinea teach them to you?"

Moses lifted an iron cauldron from one of the crates. "No, ma'am. Dulcie don't hold with no religion. She got to go to the master's service in the big house. It didn't take. But I never stop prayin' for her."

How could even a freed black man believe?

Oona pushed aside the flannel shirts she'd been pricing. "How do you do it?" she burst out. "How can you live in a world where you aren't wanted?"

Moses met her stare. "Because livin' without hope is worse. And because this here world is not my home."

They both cocked their heads at the sound of screams from the half-open door. A loose horse? A drunk from Petersen's bar?

"Just children having fun," Oona said brightly. But Moses shook his head and put down his pry bar.

"I don't think so, Miss Oona."

A group of boys gathered at the edge of the square under the gray clouds of yet another storm. Since Caroline had been fired, the children who didn't attend her mercantile school were running wild. No one else had stepped forward to take her place. A tall youth, one who would have been an eighth-grader if there had been a school teacher to teach them, held a smaller child upside down by his feet. The younger boy was Elijah, Moses's son, but he was silent. The scream came from his friend Zebulun Wilkins.

Zeb shoved his way into the circle of jeering youths, battering the older boys with his small fists. One of the largest, the Davis boy, turned and knocked him on his back with one careless arm. Zeb slipped and, arms flailing, went down in the mud.

Moses skidded to a stop at the edge of the group. "Boys, is something wrong?" he asked in an easy manner. Too easy.

Their mocking glances passed over him and back to his son, who dangled like a loose branch from the older child's big hands.

Well, they'd listen to Oona. She'd been a big sister long enough. "Stop that right now. Put Elijah down. You know better, Simon Merrill. And you, George Davis. Have you nothing better to do?"

The Merrill boy gave her a dirty look but complied. He flipped Elijah and set him on his feet. "What's it to you, lady? Just another colored kid."

"We was just havin' a little fun," the Davis boy said, his whine at odds with an already-changed voice.

"If this is your idea of fun, it won't be when I tell your parents. You should be in the woods helping your fathers. Not bothering younger children." And especially not this one. She straightened the collar of Elijah's flannel shirt, re-buckled the strap of his overalls. His dark eyes were wide, and he trembled as much as she did. "Go on home, boys. All of you. And find something useful to do, or your parents will find it for you."

They went, shuffling their feet and muttering, casting glances over their shoulders.

Zeb patted his friend on the back. "I tried to help, 'Lijah. I tried."

Oona sighed. "You did well, Zebulun. But next time come and get an adult."

"They didn't mean nothing." Elijah sounded as though he was trying to convince himself.

Moses looked down at his feet. "They listened to a white woman but not to me."

Oona shrugged, though she felt anything but dismissive. "I'm one of nine children. Five of them were brothers, and one of those was Michael. I had to learn to fight."

"I'm all right." Elijah drew himself up to his full height. Lanky like his father, a full inch taller than his best friend. "Thanks, Zeb. Thanks, Miss Oona."

"You go on, too." Moses had found his father voice. "Go home and help your mama, and don't go out in the square again today. Do your lessons. And Zebulun, you go on home, too."

The dryness had lasted just until the wagons were unloaded. Now a needle-like rain fell outside, and shadows gathered in the corners.

Oona lit a lamp before she and Moses took on the shipment again. He pried the tops off crates, and she followed, checking the items against her list: sugar, tea, coffee, tin cups and plates, pocket knives and bullets, and two crates of rather ugly fabric, but it beat taking old dresses apart.

There was no more singing.

The rain cleared by supper time, revealing a dusky purple twilight. This was a pretty enough country if one didn't have to live here.

After her nightly super with Pace, Oona made her way back to the hotel. From the kitchen, she saw a light burning in the livery stable. She drew closer and placed her dirty dishes on a log. Was Michael working late tonight? Mayhap she could talk to him, convince him to convince Caroline not to teach the Jacksons. For theirs, and everyone else's safety.

It was possible, wasn't it?

About as possible as Michael convincing her not to go back to Ireland, or her persuading him to go with her.

She followed a lantern's glow to one of the rear stalls where her brother sat on a bale of hay and stroked an upright but still-shaky foal, as its dam looked on with an anxious air. He lifted a beaming face to her. "Look, Oona. 'Tis a strong baby boy, and Flossie here did a fine job."

Oona couldn't help smiling. Michael had always loved baby anythings, had assisted with foaling and lambing and calving from the age of ten. Good thing Caroline was expecting. Oona knew the kind of father Michael would be.

She knelt beside him in the hay and fell silent for a few minutes, lost in the wonder of new life. They could almost have been children on the tenant farm back home. Those times were so painful and yet, from this vantage point, so innocent.

"I heard about what happened in the square." Michael kept his voice hushed though they were the only people in the barn.

"Who? How? Surely not the big boys. They'd be too embarrassed. Surely not Moses or Elijah."

185

"No. Zebulun Wilkins has a big mouth. He's been braggin' around town about how Miss Oona stood up to the bullies."

"Well, 'Miss Oona' shouldn't have had to."

" 'Tis a nasty business all around."

They sat on, taking turns petting the foal as the oil lamp cast its glow from a metal hook. She had always had a special bond with this brother, the wild seed of the Moriartys, who had done and gotten away with things she'd only dared to think about. If she'd been a man, she would have been like him. Heaven help a world with two of them.

"Caroline found another note."

"Oh, Michael, no." Whatever her brother was now, he did not deserve this.

"This one was on the door of our cabin."

"Michael, you cannot let this continue."

"Do you not think I know that, lass? 'Tis the right thing to do, but we knew it wouldn't be easy."

"Could she not — could she not teach Elijah and Deborah privately? In their home? Or yours?"

Michael shot her a look. The blue eyes, so like her own, had hardened. "She could. And she very well may if this gets much worse. But it would be like — like —"

"Like giving in," she finished.

Like being back home.

Time for something a little lighter. "How did you and Caroline meet? You never did tell me."

Michael started a little, and something in his face tightened. "Back in Ohio, when I was living with Uncle James. She — married my best friend. You've heard me speak of Dan, so you have. Danny died and she joined the wagon train as a cook. So I — we —" He spread his big hands helplessly. "You know."

Oona did know more than Michael realized. She'd always been able to catch him in a lie, a half-truth or an evasion. Which was this? There was more to his story. In time, she'd sort it out.

"I am surprised you decided to stay here," she said. "You never cared much for farming."

" 'Tis true. But I need to make a home for Caroline. She's been through so much. I've seen the land. Anyone can grow anything here. And Jenny wants me to help her with her horse breedin', so I'll be busy enough."

"What did you want to do?" she pressed. "Before Caroline came along?" The Caroline who had tamed Michael, and kept him from helping Oona get justice for their people.

187

"I had thought about ranching," Michael said slowly. "There's prime land nearly for the taking out along the Colorado River. Scouted out a few parcels before I gave up the trail. But it's even more remote than this place, and I can't uproot her again."

Michael loved this woman, more probably than he had ever loved anyone. Had he ever put anyone first, given up something he really wanted? He'd been kind to people, good to people, but always out of the overflow. This West had changed him more than he knew.

"Will you be stayin' here? With Pace?"

She was silent for a minute. "You know what I have to do. When I come back, well, then we'll see."

Michael slammed a fist against the wall. "You're still planning to do that?"

"Someone has to." And 'twould not be him.

"You'll look for Tom." It was no longer a question.

"And Caitrin and the littles. I promise, Michael. And I'll tell them where you are, and you can bring them here."

Where the littles could run barefoot and fish in the creek and eat their fill, even if it was just beans and dried meat. Where they could get roses in their cheeks again. Where

Caitrin could find a future. She'd be a young woman now. And Tom could farm to his heart's content on his own land at last. Pace and Tom would get along. Both men of few words, but they made every word count.

Michael stretched and yawned. "Will ye be coming out to the cabin tomorrow? I want to show Caroline what we've done."

"The store closes at three on Saturdays."

"That should give us enough time. Pace is coming, and Caroline insists on packing a picnic supper." He paused for a beat. "Women."

Men.

17

Oona braced herself as the spring-less wagon bounced over what passed for a trail. "Are we almost there?" she murmured to Pace.

His eyes crinkled at the corners, and he squeezed her hand. "Ain't that rough. Remember how it was before."

She knew she shouldn't complain. This trail hadn't even existed the last time she'd visited Michael's claim. Michael and Pace carved it out of the woods from the dozens of trees they'd felled for Michael's new home. It was wide enough for the buckboard Michael had made out of an old prairie schooner and wide enough for the horse to draw them through the thick trees. No wider than it needed to be.

Oh, what a beautiful world, with the trees stretching to a blue, blue sky and the first wild flowers poking through the leaves. How full and fruitful this Oregon Country was.

With Pace beside her they were on their way to see the progress Michael had made on his log home, working nights and weekends, sometimes with Pace at his side to help clear the wilderness.

"I could do this for us," Pace said in a voice so low only she could hear. "Stake me a claim, build us a cabin. Ain't that hard."

How, how could she leave this man? Oona rested her head on his shoulder. "When I come back."

Michael pulled the horse to a stop just before their clearing, jumped down, and offered Caroline his hand. As she gathered her skirts, Oona saw Caroline look over her shoulder, and saw the joy drain from her face. Oona followed her gaze.

"Michael." Caroline's voice was little more than a thread.

"It will look better when we get the chinking in, but you can see —"

"Michael!"

Michael turned from picketing the horse. "What?" He followed his wife's gaze. Then a strangled sound broke the silence of the clearing.

A pile of burned logs leaned crazily in every direction — all that was left of their beautiful two-story log home. Charred lengths of wood were flattened to the ground where the walls once stood. The window holes had caved in, the entire house a pile of rubble. Only the chimney still stood, mocking them with its wholeness.

The smoke still hung in the air above the cabin, not drifting in the still air, and Oona coughed. Pace handed her his bandana, and she covered her mouth.

"Who . . . ? What?"

Beside her, Pace struggled for words.

Another primitive howl came from her brother's lips.

Who had done this? How could they have done it? And why?

All his hard work, his and Pace's. Nights and weekends after their other jobs. Log by log, felled, notched, assembled. Calluses on their already-callused hands.

Caroline had bragged about not being sick for her entire pregnancy. She was sick now. She ran to the edge of the woods and vomited tiredly into the dead leaves. Michael went to hold her head, and when she was done, he wiped her mouth with his bandana.

The sun went behind a cloud, and Oona pulled her shawl closer. "Who could have done this?" she burst out. Who would hate them, generous Michael and gentle Caroline, that much?

"I do not know." Her brother began to

pace, his long legs kicking up the blackened wood scraps. "Mayhap the person who left the notes. Doesn't matter. I will kill whoever did this. I will kill them."

"No, Michael. You won't." Caroline, faint but firm, clung to the side of the buckboard.

"Maybe — maybe you can rebuild. I can help . . ." Oona would pound nails, would do anything to take that hopelessness from her brother's face. And the anger.

Michael scuffed his boot in the ground then picked up a piece of charred wood and flung it across the clearing. " 'Tis no good. They'll just come back. Maybe they'll burn the crops next time or poison the stock."

It was starting to rain, great fat drops from the now-leaden sky, and Michael swept Caroline into his arms. "I'm taking you home. We'll sort this out there."

They parted in the square, Mike shielding Caroline as though she'd shatter into a million pieces. Their rickety door shut on its one squeaking hinge.

Pace turned to Oona, took off his hat, and raked his hand through his cropped hair. "I can help him rebuild."

"Why would he want to?"

"Why? Because this is his home, now."

"This is your West."

She was shivering, and Pace drew her close despite what anyone saw, what anyone said. "Shh. It's all right, Oona. It ain't always like this. People got to be, well, educated. I worked with coloreds at —" Well, at his dozens of jobs. "They ain't no different from anyone else."

"My family wasn't any different from anyone else. In Ireland. When the landlord's son died, his blood was the same color as ours."

If only she'd cry. If only she'd be like other women. But those deep blue eyes held a look of anger, of resolve, that he'd come to fear more than her tears.

They both looked up as Jenny crossed the square, moving at a pretty good clip with a covered dish in her hands. At a nod from Pace, she veered off course. "How was the cabin?"

He exchanged a quick glance with Oona. Not their story to tell. "We come back early," Pace said. "Rainin'," he added unnecessarily. "Where you off to?"

Jenny tucked a towel more securely around the steaming casserole. "Molly's sendin' this over to Miz Hale's house. Not that she'll feel like eatin', but that don't take care of the rest of the family."

"What's wrong? Did Charlie have an ac-

194

cident in the woods?"

"Nope. Miz Hale went into labor last night. She's poorly, and the baby didn't live."

"Too early?"

"Nope, right on time. To the day. Almost to the minute. Miz Foster midwifed her. Word is it was the damp in the cabin. Little guy couldn't breathe." Jenny was off again.

Pace and Oona stood rooted to their spot.

A baby dead, a mother not well. All for the lack of light and air. Would Caroline's baby, or *Caroline,* survive in one of these run-down shacks?

And who was to say their unseen enemy wouldn't try again, or wouldn't try something else?

This was his West.

Oona thrashed around the narrow room she shared with Jenny. What had possessed her to come here? Nothing had changed. This West, a place where well-meaning people had their homes burned just because they saw past the color of someone's skin.

She might as well have stayed in Ireland, lived out her life in the convent, sought forgiveness and atonement through the ancient Benedictine rituals, cleaned the stone floors until they glistened and her sins were scrubbed away. Be as safe as an Irish-woman could be in Ireland. But she ran a hand over her lips, remembered Pace's brief parting kiss — a brush of his lips to hers that promised so much more. She couldn't have both.

Could they start over again somewhere else? Some place that meant nothing to either of them?

"Well, I hope that God of yours don't fall over in a dead faint."

"He's seen worse than you, Pace. Myself, for one." Mike grinned as they maneuvered the last bench into place. He rubbed his hands together and looked around the dining room of the Hall's Mill Inn. "Why did you decide to come to church anyway?"

Pace gestured to the one window and the sheets of rain falling outside. "Ain't ridin' today. And I'm hopin' Caroline will invite me to lunch."

Mike clapped him on the shoulder. "She would have anyway."

Pace settled himself on one of the back-less benches Mike had hammered together from a broken prairie schooner. He had never been to Mike and Caroline's Sunday service, never even been curious. Left well enough alone. But today it wasn't just the rain. The whole settlement was buzzing about the Moriarty cabin, now a charred wreck in the woods. Would Mike refer to it in the sermon he'd painstakingly written? He'd told Pace about the writing, how he had to really read the Scriptures to make sure he was saying things properly. How Caroline listened to him practice, helping him to say the right words.

Mike seemed happy today, happier than one would expect in a man who'd seen his home burned to the ground. And Caroline, in the brief glimpse Pace had had of her, showed her usual serenity. Must have been some talk they'd had last night. Or was it their religion?

People began to straggle in. A couple of loggers, in town for Sunday breakfast and with nothing to do 'til the saloon opened at one. Joe and Lucy Foster and their brood, filing in quietly, keeping to themselves. Prissy Mrs. Wilkins, the one who had given Caroline such a hard time back in Ohio, and her husband and their two kids.

Jenny flashed him one of her quick grins as she settled on a bench near the back. Oh, she must be bored to come to a religious service.

And Oona, looking ragged, taking a spot well away from anyone. Had she slept at all?

He sure hadn't. He'd replayed the trip to Mike's claim, wondering who could have done it. And reliving his last brief kiss with Oona. Something he did way too often.

She was wearing her blue dress today, dark blue like her eyes, with her white shawl over her shoulders and her smoky black hair swept up with pins, almost weighing down her neck. What if he were to cross the room, sweep her up in his arms, pull the pins from that mass of black hair, and kiss her until she felt faint? Would she admit what they both wanted? Or would she bolt? No, even he wouldn't do that in a church service. Especially a church service run by his best friends.

They began with a couple of songs, Mike's rich baritone leading them off. There were no hymnals but these were songs even the heathen Pace had heard, "Amazing Grace" and "A Mighty Fortress." No piano or organ and the voices were all over the place, but at least they sang. Mike read from the Bible, something he called the Psalms.

Pace took his word for it. He'd never owned one of the things, although he knew some Scripture from the nuns teaching him to memorize passages.

Would there be a sermon? Would Mike chew out his neighbors for a fire that had

almost certainly been set?

But when the Bible reading and a short prayer were done, Mike spoke on how the Bible taught about love thy neighbor. His words were making sense and a few people in the audience seemed to be squirming a little.

Pace's gaze sharpened, wondering if someone in this crowd had burned the Moriarty cabin. They surely hadn't loved their neighbor then.

At the end of his sermon, Mike opened his arms. "For those who feel the need, you can come up and confess to me privately so I can pray for you, or you can talk to your neighbors about what's bothering you."

Caroline stood.

The crowd murmured a little.

Even Pace knew that women generally didn't speak up in church. But he vaguely recalled someone talking about an "altar call" on one of the wagon train church days held out on the prairie under open sky. Sometimes after a sermon, women had gone forward to talk quietly to whoever was the minister on the trail or to confess a sin to the group at large. A few had even gone up to be baptized if they were near a river or creek.

Caroline took a chair at the front, faced

the crowd and smiled. "It's good to see you all," she said in her quiet way. Quiet but firm, as if they were her school kids. "I'll tell you a story. Once upon a time, a little girl read her share of fairy tales, and she dreamed of her own prince. She did meet her prince, in an adventure in a strange new land. She fell deeply in love with him, and he with her." She smiled over at Mike, and he returned the smile as though some kind of a wave passed between them.

No. Pace gripped the sides of the bench. Not that story. He — and the awful Mrs. Wilkins — were the only people in the settlement who knew what had really happened back in Ohio.

Why was she doing this?

Because they had nothing left to lose.

Caroline went on, as calm as if she were dishing out beans. "The young woman and her young man couldn't wait, and they made a big mistake outside of marriage. The biggest one. And the young woman made an even bigger one: she didn't tell the young man about their baby. So the man went off and the woman stayed where she was to face the scorn of her town."

Pace took a quick glance around the room.

Miz Wilkins had sat up straight, like a pointer dog.

Lucy Foster gazed anxiously at her children. Pace could almost see her hands going over her daughters' ears.

And Oona, her mouth hung open. Well, she had to find out sooner or later. He wasn't sure if this was sooner, later, or something worse.

Caroline went on, like a charging bull but quieter. "Was the girl sorry for what she did? She was sorry she got caught. Sorry how it ended up. Another boy offered to marry her, to give the baby a name, and she accepted. He took her shame on him. He did it gladly." Caroline paused.

One could have heard a ten-penny nail drop if there were any spare nails in Hall's Mill.

"The baby didn't live. It wasn't a punishment. It happens sometimes. But the young woman couldn't let go of her shame. The guilt — it almost destroyed her."

Oona's hands were clutching the bench, her knuckles white with the effort.

But Pace's gaze traveled beyond her to Jenny. Jenny, seated on the edge of the bench, her face alive with something he didn't even pretend to understand.

What was happening here?

The rain slid past the window, the one window that looked grimy no matter how much Jenny or Oona polished it.

A pot clanged in the kitchen, Molly starting Sunday lunch, was the only sound.

"She had no friends left in that town. Nobody but her young husband. But he introduced her to his best Friend, Jesus Christ. He told her how Christ took her shame on Him, how He did it gladly, how it was a gift she could never repay. How she could invite Christ into her life, and live with Him instead of in fear of Him."

Michael crossed the room, stood behind her with one hand on her shoulder, and Caroline gave him a quick smile. "The girl was me, and her prince was Michael. God helped us find each other again on the trail, and He gave us back what we'd lost."

The smell of browning meat came from the kitchen, but Pace wasn't hungry. He scratched his neck again. That was enough. Wasn't it? Could they sing another song or — or something?

Nope, not that blessed.

Caroline gazed out at the small crowd. "You all survived the trail to get here, to get to Oregon Country, and that took will. Determination. But your own will can only get you so far. My first husband's marrying me only took me so far. It gave me a name, would have given the baby a name, protected me in that town — but it couldn't do a thing about my guilt. My shame."

She paused and a sweet smile lit her face, unlike anything Pace had ever seen on her.

"We all have some shame in our backgrounds. It can be private or public, but we have it. Jesus Christ died for my sins and yours. He paid our debts. You can hand your guilt over to Him today. You can get rid of that shame. Give Him that burden. It's too heavy for you; it always will be. If you want to come to the front, Michael will pray with you."

Well, she'd done it. Admitted to the entire settlement that she and Mike had been lovers back East before her first marriage.

Pace had to admit that took nerve. It would probably get their second house burned to the ground, but . . .

The room was silent, too silent. How did one end something like this? He knew what he wanted to do, light out of there as soon as possible. But he felt compelled to stay with his friends. Besides, no God could handle Pace Williams' guilt.

A bench scraped back and every head in the room swiveled toward it.

Jenny Thatcher stood up tall and proud and made her way to the front of the room. Her head, with its growing out blonde hair was held high, and her gaze was only for Caroline and Mike. "I got guilt even you don't know about," Jenny told her friends. "You think that'd work for me?"

He found Oona in the back of the inn, huddled in the doorway that led out to the loading dock, staring out at the cold steady rain. She had her arms wrapped around her and he added his, just to give them both a little warmth. "That was somethin', wasn't it?" he murmured into her hair. "Jenny got religion."

Oona swiveled just enough to look up at him. " 'Tis a wonderful day, Pace. I'm glad to learn my sister-in-law wasn't as perfect as she seemed. I know that sounds mean, but I . . . was afraid I'd never live up to her calmness. No matter what happens, she's serene, even after the shock of her home being burned down. She smiled at those people in church. They are still her friends. Even after what she confessed."

He looked down into that beautiful, hard face. And saw the pain beneath the bluster. If only he could heal this woman he loved so much.

But Caroline had saved his life, saved all their lives, in the Blue Mountains. He owed her still, a debt he could never repay, not that Caroline would hold him to it. He held it to himself. "She was a young girl," he said. "She was in love and thought it would be all right because she and Mike would make it right. And don't forget, part of it was Mike's fault."

"That's been Michael's fault all his life."

"Anyone can fall from grace, in that way, and others." If only she knew how hard it was for him to keep his hands off her, in those brief hours in his cabin.

"I do not understand this place." Oona's gaze had turned back to the rain.

"Well," he said from a suddenly dry throat. "You won't have to understand it much longer."

He wrapped his arms around her more tightly, and they stared out at the falling rain.

18

Though the café was crowded with Sunday breakfasters, Pace separated Oona's musical brogue from the din. He watched out of the corner of his eye as she approached a tableful of loggers. "May I get you anything else, gentlemen?"

"Depends. Are you on the menu?" Victor Curtis asked.

Pace's fingers tightened around his tin mug. He started to push back his chair.

But Oona beat him to it, tossing her hair and turning away. "Faith, and haven't I turned the stomach of every man who's known me?"

The loggers slapped each other on the back and roared, and even Curtis parted with a reluctant smile.

Pace forked up the last of his Sunday morning hotcakes.

Victor's dark gaze followed Oona's every move as she served breakfast. Pace didn't like the way the man looked at Oona, but then he didn't like Curtis anyway. The man was worse with Caroline, harassing not only a married woman but an expectin' one, and always when Mike was out of the picture. That would come to a head eventually, and Pace didn't want to be there when it did. But most likely he would be.

And Oona should not be here. Not in this place, where men starved for women looked at her as though she were some kind of prize. She should be in her own home, tending her own family, doing the little things and the big things that made up a woman's day. She'd handled the loggers today, but as they'd learned with Bennett, it only took once.

Could Pace keep her safe? He could, but it wasn't likely he'd get the chance.

Their glances met over a man's head, and she gave him a fleeting smile. "Later?" she mouthed.

Pace nodded. Later.

He found Jenny in the kitchen, washing dishes as Sadie dried. As she worked, Jenny sang the ancient ballad of "Barb'ry Allen." Was that a glimmer of interest in Sadie's eyes? Hard to tell. He palmed a leftover biscuit and waited 'til the song was over. "We ridin' today?"

He and Jenny still rode on Sundays.

Oona waved them off. "I'd hold you back, so I would — I can ride, but not like you two. I'll take my nap, and I'll be fresh for you in the evening."

Oona trusted him with Jenny, the second-most beautiful woman in the settlement. She was that secure in his love.

If only he were that secure in hers.

Jenny dried her hands and winked at Sadie. "I got church first. I can go right after the service is done. Take me ten minutes to change."

Jenny was religious now, sitting prim and pretty on the backless benches, following along in a secondhand Bible, even writin' stuff down on a piece of paper. Jenny's language cleaned up and something was drawn out of her, like one sucked poison out of a snake. She didn't preach to anybody. She didn't have to.

Could he do it? No, not even for Mike and Caroline.

God had left Pace Williams alone since his eleventh year. Seemed they were both fine with that.

Pace helped himself to another cup of coffee but drank it out on the back loading dock while Jenny went to Mike and Caroline's service. He wasn't that bored. He saddled both horses while he waited, and Jenny went to her room and changed out of her waitress duds into pants and a shirt. The other women in the village raised their eyebrows, he was sure of that. But compared to everything else she'd done, wearing dungarees didn't amount to much. Easier to ride that way, and Jenny was all about riding.

She rode in front of him, her back straight, as they headed out toward Barlow Camp. The trees surrounded them, a thick uncut vastness of pine and spruce. The air smelled of new growth and mud. He knew she was just waitin' to give Rebel his head, to streak across some open space the way she'd torn across the prairie. He didn't know what drove her. Prob'ly the same things that drove him: the need to keep going. To outrun whatever past she had, and Jenny's was considerable.

But Jenny, now, she'd changed. Started changing on the trail, showing both a tough side and a soft side he'd never seen in her. Blossomed under Caroline's friendship, and gained confidence helping him on the wagon train and now in her hotel job. She wasn't the woman he'd known in St. Joe. And now, going to what passed for church in this place, she'd moved even further from the old Jenny. She seemed — happy. At peace. Ready for something. It'd be nice if Jenny could find a man, someone who could — well, Jenny didn't need supportin'. Maybe they could support each other.

He chuckled to himself. *Matchmakin'.* He'd have to remember to tell Oona.

He owed Jenny; she'd pushed him to Oona, who would be leaving. He counted each bright day, each moment, huddled over a checkerboard, reading aloud from Caroline's month-old newspapers, sharing a meal. Would each time be the last? Would he think one day, "I'll have to tell Oona that," and realize he couldn't?

Oona said she'd come back. But what was there to come back to? A drifter with a past. A formerly unwanted child, now an unwanted man. He had some money saved up. He could take care of her, but Oona wasn't about wealth. Would she still love him if she knew everything?

He knew what Jenny had been, knew what Caroline and Mike had been. But none of them knew what he had been, and best to leave it that way.

As they rode single file through the forest, Pace let Jenny take the lead. Weren't a whole lot of open places to ride through around here, and he had to admit he missed the prairie, missed giving Prince his head. But these forests took his breath away. So vast, so silent, so ancient. Despite man's inroads, still so powerful. Pace and Jenny stopped once, by mutual consent, to gaze on a single deer. The doe looked up, stared at them, then loped gracefully back into the forest. She would share her place with them.

They rode on, under a canopy of trees that shut out the light. These woods were different from any he'd known with their gnarled ancient trees and the damp moss under foot. Moisture dripped from the leaves, even on a dry day. Sounds came from the plodding hooves and a bird's trill. Pace always felt that he wasn't alone, that there was something out there even beyond the woodland creatures. Something he wasn't sure he liked.

A twig cracked somewhere, and Rebel reared up. Jenny reached out to pat his mane. "There, boy."

Rebel didn't spook easily, and neither did Jenny. She wasn't spooked now. But like Pace, she respected these woods.

A red fox that had probably stepped on the twig came out into the open.

When Jenny came out into a clearing, Pace drew alongside her. "How far you wanna go?"

"Let's go to the creek, same's we did last week, and then head back. If we time it right, Caroline will have supper on."

Pace nodded. "When we get back, I'll fetch Oona, and you can go change. Race you to the creek!" Pace started to pull ahead of her, and then he reined Prince to a sudden stop.

Jenny drew up beside them. "What is it?"

She followed his gaze to the branch of a fir tree, just over their heads. A faded scrap of blue plaid fabric fluttered from the limb.

It couldn't be. Not after all this time. But if it was, "they" sure knew how to hurt him.

Jenny took a deep breath. "Yeah. So? It's just a rag."

"Ain't so."

"Mebbe some woman was riding, and her skirt got caught."

"It's too high. And ain't no one I know got a dress like that." No one here, anyway.

Jenny had never shown fear, not when they'd fought the cholera, not when the company mutinied against them, not even in the showdown in the Blue Mountains. But he could see that whatever she saw in his face scared her now, and she reached out and put a hand on his sleeve. "Let's go back. Gonna rain anyway, and as I said

212

before, if we time it right, Caroline will have supper on. Oona'll be up from her nap now. Let's go back, Pace."

He came back to the present and gave her a small smile. "Yeah. Don't know what I was thinkin'. Let's go back."

Pace rode onward as Prince jogged behind Jenny and Rebel on the narrow trail. He didn't want to talk no more. Didn't want to think either, but he didn't have a choice in that one. It was just a piece of cloth. Wasn't it? Lots of women had blue plaid dresses; lots of men had blue plaid shirts. It didn't mean anything. He'd traveled long and far to have it not mean anything.

Nineteen years. Though he was nineteen years out from anything they could do to him, he grabbed the pommel of his saddle, trusting Prince to carry him. His knuckles turned white.

They couldn't get to him here.

19

"Well, now, ain't that pretty."

Pace reined in Prince just long enough to
admire a mountain stream still swollen from
the winter snows and rushing its way over
rocks. The sun just hit the tops of the cur-
rents, pouring down from a break in the
trees. It would be a good spot for a cabin. If
only Oona could see it.

Be nice if these trails were wider. He'd
love to give Prince his head, to canter and
trot and run. It would get him back to Oona
faster, make the most of the time they had
left. But she would be waiting. Now it was
Oona, not Jenny, who brought his supper
and stayed to talk. They kept three or four
feet between them, and she didn't stay long,
which suited Pace fine. He'd rather die than
sully her reputation.

The dinners gave them the time, and the
distance, to get to know each other. She told
him of Ireland. He told the safe, funny

stories from all the places he'd been. From the life he'd created for himself.

They hadn't set a date yet, and he didn't know how they could.

She still talked about going back to Ireland. She still asked him to go with her, about every other day. She'd saved every penny of her hotel pay, saved every cent from the mercantile, and had taken odd jobs doing laundry for the bachelor loggers. It still wasn't enough.

He found himself hoping she'd never raise the money she needed. Was that wrong? No. He needed her here, wanted her here, not avenging Kevin's death or tempting fate with her own.

He'd never thought anyone could love him, after Bernadette. Why would they?

But Oona did, in an even more complete way than Bernadette had. The man-and-woman way.

Prince stopped abruptly and whinnied.

Pace leaned over the pommel. "What is it, boy? What you got there?"

A body lay across the trail, and Pace sucked in his breath. A man, from all indications, small and thin, his wide-brimmed hat flung to one side, and a trickle of black blood from his stomach. Pace's own stomach clenched as he leaped down from Prince.

He'd seen death dozens of times. Always worse when one knew the person dying. He cradled the youth. "Jean-Luc. What are you doing way out here? Why ain't you at Fort Hall?"

The boy was lucid, but fading fast. Pace knew the signs. "I come to find you," the boy gasped. "Two men — mean 'uns — they stabbed Jacob. And they're lookin' for you."

Jacob Schwartz, the jovial trading post merchant he'd known for years and visited with every trip west. No time to mourn. If the Schwartzes had sent Jean-Luc, they had a reason. "Did Tessie send you? What'd they look like? Was they the ones who plugged you?"

"I — they —"

Jean-Luc's eyes rolled back in his head. Pace heard the too-familiar rattle. Then the boy went limp.

Pace cradled the boy in his arms and steeled himself against the sight and smell of blood. He'd met the kid several times on his trail trips. Jean-Luc was — had been — fifteen or sixteen, a wiry mixed-breed who ran errands between the Army posts and trading posts, on a paint pony almost as fast as Jenny's Rebel.

Not any more.

They were here. Nobody else would have tracked him this far after all these years or would have cared. He'd made enemies over the years, sure. Gotten on the wrong side of people. But most of it had been pretty cut and dried. Nobody else hated him this much.

Oona. He had to get her out of here. He knew what "they" could do, especially to a woman. She'd be safer even in Ireland. He didn't know what Ireland was like, beyond the stories.

But he knew Roy and Carl like a book.

"I do not understand." Oona stared at the pouch of coins, gave it an experimental heft. It was heavy and she flexed her wrist.

Pace sighed and braced himself for more explaining. Nothing was ever easy with Oona.

"Why did you change your mind? You didn't want to go, and you didn't want me to go. What happened, Pace?"

He couldn't fool this one. But he could try. Give her a half-truth and hope she took it. The half he could spare.

They'd been at it for an hour, him leaning on the counter at the mercantile, her scrubbing the same spot of splintery wood 'til it

217

glistened, breaking off their argument whenever a customer entered.

Pace hadn't expected it to be this hard. He repeated his case. "I think you should go back. Not to fight the English, but to find your brother and the rest of your family. And I'll help. I just got — some business to finish here first. Then I'll catch up."

"Do they have wagon trains going east?"

Pace counted to ten. "No. Viola and Steve Miller are riding out to the mission. They want to see the Whitmans one more time before Vi gets — tied to the house." He meant pregnant, but a fellow didn't say that word even to his fiancée. If Oona still was his betrothed. He took up the thread again, hastily. "There's always someone headin' back east from the Whitman place. They'll take you to Fort Hall, and you can get a military escort from there."

Oona folded her arms in that mulish stance he had come to know well. "I could also wait at the mission and Reverend Whitman could marry us when you got there. Then we could ride east together. I could help Mrs. Whitman with the little ones. I am in no hurry, Pace."

Well, good for her. He was.

Her plan would have been fine if they had been two ordinary people, two normal people. But Oona anywhere in Oregon Country wasn't good enough. He wanted her out of here.

Though he had given Jean-Luc a quick burial in the woods, the image of the boy's mangled body haunted him. That was what Roy and Carl could do, and they didn't even know Jean-Luc. What would they do to Pace or to get back at Pace? He'd rather face Roy and Carl alone.

He took her face in his hands. "Oona, I promise I'll catch up to you. Prince is fast, and he knows these mountains and plains. Without a wagon train to worry about, I can make Fort Hall in a couple weeks. I'll catch up, and we'll go to Ireland together." If he lived.

"And what will I ride? I don't have a horse."

Pace drew a deep breath. *Sorry, Jean-Luc.* "There's a fast, little paint pony I found wanderin' in the woods. Be perfect for you." And, he hoped, better luck than he'd been for the courier.

Oona squirmed under his touch. "Pace, are you memorizing my face?"

He was. The full lips, the high cheekbones, the blue eyes that could gleam with laughter or look into places he wasn't ready for her to go. He stared at the wisps of black hair framing her face, curling their way out of the braid. He admired the courage, the passion, the gentleness. All that was Oona. He covered his sorrow with a laugh. " 'Course not. I just like lookin' at you."

"And I, you." Her smile warmed him. But then she shoved the pouch of coins across the counter. "I cannot take your money."

He moistened his lips. She had to. "Sure ya can. I got no need of it here."

"But this is for your homestead!"

"Won't be no homestead without you." That part, at least, was true. He pressed her hand around the bag. "Take it, Oona. Ain't for you. It's for us." In more ways than she knew. He could tell she was wavering, tell also that even she was tired of the hour of arguing.

"You'll catch up?" Her voice trembled like a little girl's.

" 'Course I will." If he could. If there was anything left of him.

He kissed her, and she clung to him. He was the one who had to break away. He fought for steadiness. "I'll go now. Got stuff to do. You be over for supper?"

" 'Course I will." She dimpled as she mimicked him, and he tried to memorize her smile.

220

■ ■ ■ ■

Oona counted the day's take. Sales had been brisk and Annie Two-Stars would be happy. She sifted the coins through her fingers, noted the amount in her ledger, and then picked up Pace's sack one more time. Must be two, three hundred dollars in here. She put the bag in her apron pocket, where it weighed down one side of the garment. Well, that was that. He was generous. She had to admit it. But why now? Why, when he'd been so opposed to her going back to her homeland?

Did he love her no longer?

No. She touched her cheeks, still warm from his caress. The hands and gaze of a man in love. And a man who moved her far more than Kevin ever had.

She was going home, and Pace was going with her. So he said. She had nothing to fear, from the landlord or anyone else. Pace would protect her. Pace could do anything, had done almost everything. She'd bank on him over anyone else. She should be glad.

But getting what she wanted wasn't as gratifying as it had looked.

20

There were no packages or messages for Pace to deliver, and it was too early for supper. Might as well stop by and see Oona. At least that's what he kept telling himself. Long as she was around, he'd keep Annie's store up and running. Single-handed.

Oona was marking figures in a ledger, and looked up too quickly when he came through the door. "Pace." Her smile transformed her, but then it always had, way before he'd learned she had a special smile for him.

She wore a plain brown dress, but she made it look better than it was, and she'd done up her hair in two braids and wrapped them around her head. The glossy blue-black ropes seemed heavy, but Oona kept her head high. Her blue eyes sparkled. "What can I do for you this fine spring day?"

It was finer with her in it.

"I'll have a — that is, do you have any —"

He spied a plateful of molasses cookies. "One of them things."

Oona slipped it into a paper sack. "That will be five cents."

He placed his nickel on the counter. She leaned her elbows on the rough wood, grinned at him, and then slid the nickel back. "I cannot charge my fiancé."

So much had passed between them. So much said, so much unsaid, so much that would never be said. He was still her fiancé, but for how long?

He nibbled the edge of the cookie. " 'S good. You make these?"

"I did. Molly let me use the hotel oven, and Annie let me sell them in here. It brings in a bit more money for —"

Her trip. Her confounded trip, which hung like a black curtain between them even on this sunny afternoon. She should have had enough money, more than enough, but she was so independent . . .

And though they talked about him catching up and going with her, only one of them knew what chance they had of that happening.

The worry must have showed on his face. Oona laughed, reached across the counter and took his hands. "Pace, Pace. Would ye indulge me in something?"

"Depends." He knew better now.

"Will ye see the sunrise with me? There's a marvelous spot atop Ryan's Hill, so there is. I want to welcome spring on a western hilltop, as far west as I can go. Before I leave. Before we leave."

"When?"

"Tomorrow morning. Will you meet me at four o'clock?"

He was doomed.

"I'll be by to go with you by three thirty."

Oona watched from the door of the mercantile as Pace crossed the settlement. He was a fine-looking man, tall and fit, thinner than Michael, but she knew the strength that lurked beneath his slimness. His cropped hair had a few flecks of silver, but it looked good on him. And she loved the way his eyes crinkled at the corners. Yes, a fine-looking man. But Pace was more than his looks. He was coming with her, against his better judgment, leaping into the cauldron that was the Irish Resistance. Would they both survive? Would they both die? Or would one go on alone? And what had caused him to change his mind?

Faith, and she was like one of the Children of Lir. Lir, lord of the sea, married his wife's sister after his wife died, and the sister,

224

Aoife, was jealous. She put a spell on the children and turned them into swans, and they were doomed to remain swans until the country heard the sound of a Christian bell. The Children of Lir were freed of the curse — 900 years later — when St. Patrick came to Ireland.

She didn't believe the myths, but she felt like a Child of Lir as she watched Pace walk away. Her past imprisoned her, and it would take more than a bell to get her out.

But she would have one sunrise with him.

Nice night. Pace walked slowly toward his cabin and dodged a group of children playing tag. Kids were staying out later now that it stayed light longer. He could go down to the creek, catch a mess of fish, and still be home before dark. Not tonight, though. He had a sunrise to watch with Oona, and he wouldn't want to oversleep.

She would ride out of these woods at the end of the week. She'd be accompanied by the newlyweds, Viola and Steve, on their way to visit Marcus and Narcissa Whitman. From there, one of the teamsters would take her to an Army post, and from there, she'd have a military escort back to the land of stagecoaches, trains, and finally, ships.

Would he catch up to her? Not from lack

of trying. But there were two of Roy and Carl and only one of him. While he wasn't an eleven-year-old kid any more, they were still Roy and Carl. The Roy and Carl who had murdered Jacob, killed little Jean-Luc just to get to him. What would they do? How long would it take? Should he have kept her here, let her face it with him? No. He loved her too much. And anyone he'd ever loved had died. Better this way because Oona would have a chance.

But he still hung around her, as often as possible.

What if she didn't survive and he did? What would he do then with the years that yawned ahead of him? Help Jenny with the horse farm? He wouldn't insult her with another offer of marriage, but he could be her business partner with separate homes and lives. Start his own place? He had the ability. Oona had his money. He'd have to start saving again.

Marry? He could do an arrangement, but only if she was a widow with kids. He wanted the whole package.

But he wanted it with Oona.

The sky over Ryan's Hill, a grassy mound a mile from Hall's Mill, was pitch black without a sliver of moon. Nobody knew who

Ryan was or what he'd done to have a hill named after him, but the settlers took advantage of the spot for their rare picnics and outings. In the daytime, they could see for miles.

Oona sat with her back against a boulder.

Pace lay on his side on the moss. It was silent, without even the song of a night bird or the skittering about of a tiny woodland creature. And it was cold. He huddled into his jacket with the sheepskin lining.

Oona's face glowed like a moonflower from within a hooded cloak.

He could take her out here, far from everyone and everything. The distance and the darkness would cover it. He'd know what it was like to hold her, to be one flesh. Fulfill the promise they both knew was there. But it would make losing her even worse. And ruin what they had left.

"Kind of pagan if you ask me," he said instead. "Like them stories you tell."

Oona laughed softly. "I don't believe the myths, Pace. I just don't want to think too deeply about Christianity."

He waited. She'd tell him when she was ready.

Oona sighed, a breath of regret in the darkness.

"I wasn't a very good novitiate, mayhap

because I never wanted to be one in the first place. Sometimes I caught glimpses of God, or a feeling, usually during the Offices — those are the services we're all required to go to several times a day. But God was elusive, and the next day, I was back to being Oona."

"I know what the Offices are, I was raised by nuns. And it ain't such a bad thing to be Oona." Pace smiled in the darkness.

"Maybe not to you. Didn't help that I was bitter about what happened with Hawthorne, what happened with Michael, losing Kevin, and my family." She leaned forward a little, and he caught her soap-and-lavender scent. "Do you know, Pace, my brothers never told Kevin? They couldn't. He would have stormed the manor house or the convent. And everything would have come crashing down around us. So Kevin had a fiancée who'd vanished into thin air."

Yeah, he'd be bitter too, especially if the fiancée was Oona. "Do you still believe in God? After everything that's been done to you?" He could talk about anything — almost — if the darkness covered him. Things he wouldn't say in daylight, or in his right mind.

"I'll always believe. I'm Catholic. And I saw great faith, and sacrifice, and devotion

in some of my sister nuns. I saw unshake-
able faith in my mother. But after what I've
been through, it's hard to believe He cares
about me."

Pace stretched out, hands behind his head,
and contemplated the still-inky sky. "Never
believed in God in the first place. Never had
a reason to." Did he want to believe? With
all his heart. He'd heard Caroline's speech,
seen the change in Mike, and the more
recent change in Jenny. Could God care for
such a one as him? Not likely. Hadn't yet,
anyway.

Oona was watching him. "Who are you,
Pace? I don't mean the jokes, the stories,
the easy way out. Who are you? And why
did you take to this life?"

"What difference does it make?"

"Pace. It matters. If we're to be married
—"

If. Even she had enough sense to realize
something could go wrong. She just didn't
know what or that there was a greater threat
even than Ireland. He had never told anyone. He had never discussed the events of
that night, not even with the other two boys.
Only on the witness stand. But he couldn't
keep secrets from this woman. He wanted
her to know him. Even if they never saw
each other again. And the darkness covered

everything. Well, most things.

Pace drew a deep breath. "I went to the orphanage when I was four." He didn't look at her. He stretched out on his back and stared up at the fading stars. "Never knew my pa, and my ma — she couldn't take care of me." Leave it at that. Lay out the facts. Be as cool as if he were discussing stops on the trail. "The nuns were strict, but mostly kind. There were a lot of rules. We got clean clothes, three meals a day, and school. Wasn't bad for an orphanage. I've heard stories. Worst part was not mattering to anyone. Until Bernadette . . ."

"Tell me." Her voice was soft, though they had no humans nearby to disturb, as though he was a horse and she didn't want to spook him.

And he owed her the truth. "Bernadette was an older girl, stayed on at the home on account of she had no place to go. She was nice. She took a couple of my pals and me under her wing. Looked like you, a little."

"Go on." It was barely a whisper.

"She was engaged." He swallowed. "To a man named Roy. He was nice when the nuns were around. He was polite and had manners. Bernadette cleaned the kitchen at night, and she'd set things up for breakfast the next morning. The nuns would go upstairs and go to bed. Me an' a couple other boys knew they'd be asleep, and we'd sneak down to be with Bernadette, help her clean. She'd give us cookies, and we'd sometimes play checkers. We weren't supposed to be up. But no one knew, because the kitchen was in the basement. Couldn't hear anything going on down there iffen you were upstairs.

"Roy found out about Bernadette being in the kitchen at night. He would come after the nuns had gone to bed. At first, he was polite. He'd sort of tease us boys, tell us we needed to go to sleep so he could be alone with Bernadette. Sometimes we went. But I sort of knew it wasn't right, so I stayed on while he was there. He'd get mad. He started showing up drunk. The little boys ran from him. But I didn't want to leave Bernadette alone. Then he started bringing Carl with him." Pace paused, thinking about the man.

Carl, who worked at the stockyards, cutting the meat from the great beasts as they swayed on their iron hooks. Carl, lean and muscled, with his too-long blond hair and those cold green eyes. Like fish eyes. Carl didn't say much. Pace didn't like Carl. Pace looked into the inky darkness, wishing he didn't have to say more. But he did.

231

"We had just finished the cleanup. Bernadette was setting up the checkerboard and
us boys were wrangling about who got to sit
where." He often wondered what had happened to Alvin and Charlie. Had they been
adopted or taken to wandering like him?
Did they remember that night in 1827? He
did, more often than he'd like to.

"Bernadette had looked especially pretty
that night in a blue plaid dress under her
white apron, a scarf of the same plaid holding back her hair. She had been given some
fabric and made the dress herself. That
night it was just the four of us until Roy
pounded in.

"Roy was drunker than I'd ever seen him.
He couldn't have walked a straight line. And
Carl was drunk and swaggerin' and giggled
when Roy upset the checkerboard. Bernadette stood up, and smoothed her dress all
nervous-like. And she said, 'Roy, this isn't
one of our nights.'

"And Roy just snorted and said, 'They're
all my nights. You belong to me. I can do
what I want.' And Bernadette tried to tell
him it was our night. And he said us boys
didn't matter and he had his mind on havin'
a little fun. I could see she was scared. She
kept twisting her hands under her apron.

"Roy's eyes glittered. 'You sayin' no to me,

woman?' he said. 'Nuh-uhn. I'm gonna have you — tonight.' Charlie and Alvin scattered. I stayed. He grabbed her arm, and said, 'It's gonna be tonight, darlin'. Here, while your precious nuns are upstairs asleep. Then you won't be nervous on our wedding day — or our wedding night.' And he laughed at her as he kissed her.

"I jumped on him and screamed at him to leave her alone. Roy swatted me off like a fly. He said that was why he brought Carl. To take care of me. Carl grabbed me, and I fought. I fought so hard. He took me to the pantry and shut the door, and I fought as hard as I could. He beat me up. Broke a couple ribs and my nose. I had black eyes for weeks. And even though I was feeling the pain of his fists, I could hear Bernadette, she was trying to scream, but it was little whimpers. Roy . . . I could hear him slapping her.

"I used to put things away for Bernadette. When Carl came at me again I grabbed the broom and slid it around his ankles. Carl fell and cracked his head on the wall, which made him dizzy, I guess. He kept blinking at me. I crawled over him and busted into the kitchen. Carl was right behind me in seconds.

"Roy and Bernadette were fighting. He

grabbed her sleeve, jerked her around, and just walloped her right across the face. She went down and her head cracked on the stone floor. He stood there for a second, holding her torn sleeve in his hand. I went for him like a tornado, beating on him with strength I didn't know I had. He flung me aside and turned to look at her.

"There was . . . blood all over, streaked on the stone floor, seeping from her head, staining the tiles she'd scrubbed that morning. Roy went over to her and bent down. 'You gettin' up?' he asked and then he had the grace to look horrified. He started yelling that he didn't mean it." Pace looked away from the stars, his gaze shifting to Oona.

Tears were running down her cheeks.

He had to look away quick, or he'd not be able to finish.

"Alvin and Charlie didn't run away. They ran upstairs and woke up Sister Mary Francis. She came running down the stairs with the boys right behind her. Roy heard her coming and grabbed Carl. They ran like the cowards they were right out the door as if their tails were on fire." Pace would remember the smell of leaf mold and blood for the rest of his life.

"There was a trial. Charlie and Alvin were

witnesses that Roy had been there. Carl was a reluctant witness. And me. I was the star witness against Roy Haskins for the murder of Bernadette."

Mother Superior had been gentle with him, buying him a new outfit for the trial, making sure treats were set aside for the nights he couldn't stomach dinner, leaving a lamp lit for the nights he couldn't sleep. She had walked him to the courthouse herself. She'd straightened his collar, tamed a lock of hair. "Just tell the truth, boy," she'd said as they walked into the courthouse. "Get justice for our beautiful Bernadette."

He remembered looking at her without speaking. Justice? Justice would have been not letting Roy court Bernadette in the first place. But then, they only saw the polite man, they didn't see Roy the mean drunk. Wasn't their fault, he supposed. They'd not known Roy was visiting in the night.

"I told the truth. Roy received an eighteen-year sentence for murder. And I packed my belongings and walked away from the orphanage the next day. I found work because I was big, almost a man. And I just went with whatever job I could, until I became a wagon master." He finally dared to look at Oona. He saw no judgment, only love.

She held out her arms. "Pace, come here." She held him as he should have been held nineteen years ago, and as the sun streaked the Eastern sky, he knew the defining difference between Oona and Bernadette.

Oona Moriarty would never be anybody's victim.

21

"There. That should do you." Pace tightened the cinch on Oona's horse one more time. The third? The fourth?

She looked down at him, regal from her perch on the paint pony, her skirts modestly arranged as she sat astride, her hair in two thick braids like the Indian women, crowned by a wide-brimmed hat. Her saddlebags bulged with the food Jenny and Caroline had pressed on her. He had groomed the horse for her, personally overseen the buying of the tack. He could at least keep her safe in this country, couldn't he?

The square was waking up, dew on the stubby grass, white webs of it hanging from the trees. The sun peeked over the horizon.

A few feet away, the Millers hugged Vi's folks and promised to be back soon. A promise neither he nor Oona could make.

"You'll catch up to me?" Oona was confident on the outside, but a hint of fear lay underneath. The scared little girl only he had glimpsed, and only briefly.

" 'Course I will." *If he could.* The reality he only dared whisper to himself.

They did not kiss. She did not reach down to hug him. Their real good-bye had been on Ryan's Hill. When he'd revealed more of himself to her than he ever had to anyone, and she'd taken it, no judging, unashamed.

"So. You have enough food, and you've got your gun." Practical matters, those were the only things that could save them. Would they meet again in this lifetime? *Don't go. Don't go.*

But she had to. For reasons even she didn't understand.

Caroline stood a few feet away, her arms clutched over her belly, tears streaking her small face. Oona hadn't wanted anything to do with her after that church service, and Caroline's heart was big enough to leap over that, to love Oona anyway.

Pace's heart only had room for Oona.

The Millers mounted their horses and turned toward the road out of town. With one last look, Oona clicked to her mount and followed them.

Pace watched until the trio was out of sight.

That was that. At least for now. How did

people do this? They didn't. He turned and headed blindly toward the saloon.

But Jenny stopped him. Jenny was dressed for work at the hotel in a shirtwaist, skirt, and apron, but leading Rebel. "He ain't been out for a couple of days," she said. "You wanna take him for a run?"

Pace cleared his throat. He would beat this, ride out the pain on the fastest horse in Oregon Country. "Yeah, sure. I'll bring 'im back when I'm done."

Whenever that was.

How had Jenny known? And why couldn't it have been Jenny he loved?

Oona scrabbled on the forest floor for a piece of dry wood. It was the least she could do. Steve Miller had started the fire, and now, while Vi mixed up biscuit dough, he was skinning the rabbit Viola had shot. They were competent people, especially Viola. Would Oona have become that capable if she'd stayed?

Vi Miller didn't try to ride in a dress, but she didn't wear pants like Jenny either. She wore a divided-skirt kind of thing that made it possible for her to ride modestly, but without yards of skirt to gather and bunch.

Oona studied the design. She could make one. It would be helpful if she came back here. When she came back here.

Pace was coming for her. They'd go to Ireland together. They'd find her family and put her other ghosts to rest. If she said it often enough . . .

What was Pace doing tonight? Had Michael and Caroline taken pity on him, invited him to supper, or was he dining with Jenny again? Was he thinking of her?

What if he were to ride through those trees, his shape taking place in this gathering dusk? Would his dark eyes be alert with the sense of purpose he had, the love for her and only her? Would he jump from the horse before Prince stopped, scoop Oona up, and kiss her until she felt faint? Would she go with him then? No, this wasn't a fairy tale and he wouldn't. She tossed her piece of wood on the blaze.

They had a pleasant supper by the campfire, talking or not as the spirit moved them. Steve stamped out the fire, Vi washed the dishes in the creek, and they spread out their bedrolls on the mossy ground. Steve and Vi fell asleep holding hands outside their cocoons.

But Oona stayed awake, alert to every noise in this forest, the hoot of an owl, the skittering of a tiny creature. The moon rose. The sky between the trees became peppered with stars. Was Pace looking at the same moon and stars back in Hall's Mill?

What was she doing here? Of all the strange things she'd done since that morning in the landlord's barn, this had to be one of the strangest. Sleeping on the ground in a forest, on the way back to a trip no sane person made twice. And without the one person who completed her soul. She had to do this for her family. Didn't she? If only Michael had come through. Would that have eased the emptiness, filled the hole? She would never know. And how did Michael do it? They were his kin too. Was he just being Michael, the last vestiges of a life lived mostly for himself? Or was there something else, something that allowed him to release the Moriartys to fate? Or to his God?

Oona turned on her side, tried to find a yielding place on the hard ground.

Michael's God. And Caroline's, and now Jenny's. How did they do it? How could they believe after all they'd been through?

Yes, what was she doing here, lying on the cold, hard ground of a forest in a place that wasn't even a country, with two strangers, pleasant strangers, but strangers nonetheless? With the man she loved fighting his own demons back in a place that barely had a name, and herself about to take on the fight of her life? She was lonelier than ever, more lonely than she had been in the convent, more lonely than she'd been in New York, or crossing the prairie.

Fighting her way across a destroyed Ireland, surviving steerage, being a servant in New York. The rigors of the overland journey. And now going back into the belly of the beast. What had it all been worth? And where was Michael's God in all this?

She carried the six revolvers in her saddlebags. Mayhap it wouldn't be enough, but it'd be a start. She would cross this continent again, cross the ocean again, and gather some fighters. She'd take down as many landlords as she could and free any rebels who hadn't already seen the noose. Then what? She couldn't return to her village. Hawthorne would find her and the cottage was gone. Tom and the youngest Moriartys had their own lives now. She would avenge her family, with or without Pace and then what?

She tried to imagine Pace in that world, what had been her world. Tried to imagine him in an Irish village and couldn't. He would never submit himself to the English. It just wasn't in him, and she didn't want it to be. If they had any future, they would have to have it here.

Oh, Pace, come and get me. Don't let me go through this alone.

But there was no reassurance, only the sound of the wind in the treetops.

Pace pushed Rebel until even the stallion was exhausted and finally stopped by a tiny jewel of a lake, high in the mountains. The sun glinted off the blue water.

Rebel lapped at the still pool and sank gracefully to the ground.

Pace sat against a cedar tree bigger around than three men and tossed his hat to the earth. He waited for his breathing to slow. It didn't. What to do next? Everything that was in him wanted to follow Oona and bring her back. But he had business here.

They were here somewhere. Jean-Luc's broken body was a testament to that. Pace wasn't a fanciful guy, but he could almost hear their voices on the wind, hear them in a rustling in the darkness.

Would they ask around or figure they already knew enough?

Jenny was running the mercantile a few hours a day when Molly could spare her. Would they hurt her to get to him? Would they hurt Mike or Caroline? Or would they head straight for Pace?

None of this was good. If only he'd sent

his friends away along with Oona. If only he'd sent half the town.

He hadn't cared this much about anybody since, well, Bernadette. He hadn't let himself. Bernadette, who'd be in her thirties now if she'd lived, probably with a passel of kids, maybe a couple of little girls who looked like her.

He picked up a rock, almost enjoying its heft in his hands, and flung it across the pond with enough power to scrape the bark off a tree. A rabbit leaped up from its hidey-hole in the grass and streaked further into the woods.

Never again.

Whatever this was now, whatever was left of it, it ended here.

22

Pace jumped down from Prince, took off his hat, and scratched his head. "Prince, this one's a new one for me. And I thought I knew these hills."

He had never heard of the Briggs Trail. But the kid from Barlow Camp swore it was there, swore two injured loggers needed vittles. Pace had two saddlebags stuffed with flour, beans, and bacon. He'd get it over with and go back to, well, nothing.

The so-called Briggs Trail was half a mile before the turn-off to Barlow. He'd delivered to Barlow a dozen times and never noticed Briggs, or never thought of it as a trail because he never thought any civilized person could live there. The tree branches tangled overhead and shut out the light with barely room for one horse. Paced guessed there could be people camping on the Briggs. He just couldn't guess why.

It was quiet, too quiet. Dampness gathered

in the air, the kind where one wished it would either rain or dry up, but that it would do *something*. Well, he wasn't here for the weather. He wasn't here for anything anymore.

He mounted Prince again and walked him through the overgrown trail, a dark passage up the side of the Klamath Mountains. The terrain was rough. He had to think, which was easier here than in town.

A red fox poked its nose through the brush, stood on delicate feet, and left as quietly as it had come. He wished he could have shown Oona, introduced her to the good and beautiful things of this land.

Oona was gone, off to the Whitman mission with Viola and Steve. He'd had Mike check the paint pony for her, and he'd checked the mount again. She'd looked like a queen, perched up on that horse with her skirts tucked around her.

She and the Millers had been gone for two weeks. Had she made it to the Whitman compound? Would she wait for him, despite what he'd told her? Probably. She wasn't real good at following orders. Should he have gone with her? Probably. But he was tired of running. Best to tough it out. He couldn't live with himself if he didn't.

And he couldn't live with Oona. Not as a

man who ran. Not with a woman who'd never run from anything, who'd crossed this vast land alone to get justice for her family and would be crossing it again.

He'd be good enough for Oona. If it was the last thing he did. And it just might be.

He pulled Prince to a halt. These woods were *too* quiet. His neck prickled with fear. Who else was out here, and what did they want besides beans and bacon?

Then he saw it.

A strip of blue plaid cloth, hanging from a fir sapling.

Another one. He caught his breath, half in a sob, and he knew.

A twig snapped and Pace reached for his gun, but the men who'd baited him were quicker. As Roy dragged him from Prince's back, Carl whipped rope around Pace's hands, securing them behind him, and then bound his legs a little looser. "So's you can walk. Nice to see ya again, boy."

"Got a name."

"Yeah, but it's a fake one. Pace? You really didn't think we'd find you?"

Roy, a graying Roy, but Roy nonetheless, turned Prince around, hauled the saddle bags filled with supplies off the horse's back, and gave him a slap on the rump. "Go on home. We wouldn't want to waste a perfectly good horse, would we?"

It took them an hour to make the walk, Pace shackled, Carl on horseback beside him, Roy bringing up the rear, the trail a little more than a footpath up a slight incline. Yeah, they were fully in the mountains now — with the drippy green trees and the silence closing in above them. They probably had more horses stashed somewhere. He moved his head side to side trying to remember details and wonderin' if he had something he could drop behind him. Then Carl laughed, reached down from his horse, and boxed his ear. "Don't bother, Williams. Or whatever your name is now. Won't be comin' out alive. 'S why we didn't blindfold you."

"This ain't gonna bring her back." His insides were like jelly, but he kept his voice steady. No way would he show fear. That was what they wanted.

Roy wore a cloth patch over one eye. But his aim was good as he flicked cigar ash on the ground. "Don't matter. I could've got another woman. It ain't gonna bring back nineteen years of my life neither. Eighteen in jail and one huntin' you. An' it won't bring back my eye. But it'll be fun." He flashed a stumpy grin. "And 'sides, not like anyone cares."

"I got friends." Didn't he?

"That big Mick and his wife? They don't need you." Roy kept up his babble with a casual, unconcerned air. "That blonde girl? She's already pullin' away. Don't you know you can never trust a loose woman?" He poked Pace with the butt of his rifle. "Didn't ya learn that from yer ma?"

"Jenny wasn't a whore. And leave — my ma — out of this."

How long had they been watching him? And what had they seen?

Carl was silent, content to let Roy deliver the verbal blows. Carl always let Roy take the lead.

"An' don't count on the Mick's sister," Roy went on. "She'll never come back. Pretty thing — looks like Bernadette, don't she? Iffen I had the time —"

Pace tamped down his anger, just barely, as he twisted in his shackles. "If you laid a finger on her —"

Roy poked him again. "Ain't likely you'd be alive to find out."

"I didn't take your eye, Haskins."

"Might as well have. Wouldn't have been in prison if it wasn't for you. An' nobody takes anything from Roy Haskins."

Pace stumbled along the path.

"Where'd you get the blue plaid from her dress?"

To both Roy and Pace, there was only one "Her."

"When I . . . left the kitchen, I had hold of the sleeve that tore." Roy snorted. "I put it in a safe place before I went to prison. Got it when I got out. Kept it near for when I found you."

An eagle swooped low. A woodpecker tapped busily on a Ponderosa pine. The sun came out and filtered through the glossy green of the pine trees. How normal it all was, how beautiful. If Pace had been with someone else. Anyone else.

His mind jumped ahead of him, figuring his moves, looking for a strategy. He'd been taken captive before, by red men and white men. He could untie most any knot, iffen he had the hands free to do it. He could make a weapon of most anything. He wasn't an eleven-year-old kid anymore.

But most likely, they knew that.

They came out in a clearing, a small pocket of land with a few pieces of gear and a stamped-out campfire. A large flat stone dominated the area. Roy nodded to Carl, who removed Pace's hand shackles. Pace lunged for Carl. Roy twisted Pace's arms behind his back. Roy had always been big and strong, but he was quick too. Must've learned some moves in prison.

Roy wrenched him on to the flat rock, and as Roy jabbered on, Carl rewrapped Pace's hands, flung one to each side, and slammed a heavy nail through the shackles to the rock.

Had Oona sold them these nails? Had her hands brushed theirs?

Oona. If he could do one thing over . . .

Carl did the same with Pace's feet, hammering away while Roy crouched beside Pace and talked. "You never was worth anything, boy. 'S what I tried to tell her. Wasting her time on you three monkeys. Your ma didn't want you, why should anyone else? You're a loser, boy."

"Kill me." There may be a Heaven; there may be a Hell. He'd take his chances over Roy and Carl.

"Nope." Roy stretched himself up and observed Carl's handiwork. "Nice."

"Nope, we're gonna have a little fun first. You're all right for now. Me and Carl, we're gonna go back to town. I'm gonna get me a woman."

23

"You go on ahead." Reining in the paint, Oona gestured to the Millers. "I'll catch up."

Steve and Viola had been good traveling companions, not all honeymoon-like, including her in their conversations, sharing supplies. They were good people. They could have been friends. If she'd been planning to stay in Hall's Mill.

But she needed a moment to herself. No turning back after this.

Waillatpu, the bustling compound the Whitmans had carved out of the wilderness was ahead. Farmland was being tilled for this summer's planting, cattle fed on stubby grass, a newborn colt stood on shaky feet. White and native workers toiled together, creating something new. These were people with different skin colors, beliefs, and traditions. It could happen. Why hadn't it happened in Hall's Mill? Or Ireland?

The view of the mission station from this

end was one few people saw: wagon masters heading back east. Freighter drivers going back for another load. Her.

What was going on back in Hall's Mill?

She squeezed her eyes shut, remembering it in spite of herself: her brother, home at last after wandering in the desert, gentle Caroline. Would Oona have a niece or nephew, and would she ever see it? Jenny, her first friend in the West, wounded Jenny who had risen above oh, so much. People she liked and people she didn't but all with the goal of making a home in this wilderness. All part of something bigger.

Pace. His deep chuckle, his eyes crinkling at the corners. The way he stood head and shoulders above other men, and not just physically.

Pace. Who had endured things most people only whispered about. Who'd made a life out of nothing. Who wanted to share that life with her.

But she had to do this first. Didn't she? No one left to avenge her people. Had to right the wrongs. It had to be her. Hadn't it?

Pace would catch up to her. Wouldn't he?

Her hands slacked on the reins, and she looked behind her, toward the trail. Were those hoof beats? Had he come after her?

No, it would be too soon.

Still listening, she plodded toward the compound.

The Whitmans came to greet Oona, Viola, and Steve. Marcus Whitman boomed a welcome. Whitman still hale, with his sleeves rolled up over muscular forearms. Narcissa following more slowly, wiping her hands on her apron as their adopted children scattered across the mission. Narcissa squinted at them until Marcus rescued her. "My dear, what a nice surprise. You remember the young couple from Hall's Mill that I married, and Miss Moriarty, Michael's sister. She came in with the freighters."

Narcissa was sharp enough and took her cue. "You're welcome here, Mr. and Mrs. Miller. And Miss Moriarty. How are your brother and his Caroline?"

"They are — well." Not the place to tell of Caroline's condition or their ordeal of championing the Jacksons. Things like that were best confided woman-to-woman, preferably over a cup of some steaming beverage. If she stayed here that long.

Steve and Viola drifted off to exclaim over the new colt.

Marcus's gaze, as sharp as his wife's was fading, focused on Oona. "And Mr. Williams? We were surprised when he didn't

254

come back through in the fall."

"He is staying in the West." Oh, how she longed to tell them Pace was her fiancé, and she loved him dearly. But there was too much to explain. How she longed for what the Whitmans had, a love that could overcome blindness and the struggles of making a life in the wilderness. They had been among the first white people to come out here, long before the trail. All they'd had was each other. But they, and their God, had built this.

Could she and Pace have built something as good? Would she ever see this powerful land again?

He'd said he'd follow her. He promised. But she, of all people, knew what happened to promises.

"Did that young man ever find Williams?" Reverend Whitman was asking.

Oona reined in her thoughts. "Young man?"

"From Fort Hall. He said he had an urgent message. He said Williams' life might be in danger."

Young man.

Message.

Danger.

Oh, Pace.

Oona swayed in the saddle, and Whitman

caught her in his still-strong arms. "Miss Moriarty?"

He gently lowered her to her feet.

"I'm all right." She would have to be.

Narcissa was offering everything she could. "Would you like to lie down? Your room is ready. A cup of tea?"

Oona drew herself up. She needed a place to think this through. "Yes, thank you. No tea, but I would like to see my room."

Narcissa took Oona's arm. Confident in her own sphere, she led Oona toward the guest quarters. "You can rest for a day or two until the freighters come through. We have everything you need."

Everything except for Pace. And answers.

When Oona closed the door to her room at the compound, she didn't rest. She walked back and forth in the narrow space, peered through the shuttered window, and arranged and rearranged the items from her saddlebags in a drawer. Could she rearrange this news as neatly?

It all made sense now. Why he'd changed his tune on Ireland. Why he'd pushed her to go east without him, the sorrow in his gaze this past month. Someone was trying to find Pace, someone from the trading post. Why would he be in danger? Who would threaten him that much? Who would threaten him so much that he'd send her away?

Oona bit her lip.

There was only one thing, one person who would make him send her back to Ireland. Only one incident in his life posed a greater risk for her than thrusting her back into the claws of the English beast. His Ryan's Hill confession and the nightmare of two men who could be dogging his life.

Oona didn't deserve him, probably never would. But Pace didn't deserve to die at the hands of a madman.

She threw items back into her saddlebag with no regard for neatness. Oona headed to the Waillatpu stables, where one of Whitman's sons had already rubbed down the paint. She thanked the boy and, when he'd gone to another chore, she tacked her horse again. And she took one revolver from her stash of five, buckled on her holster, and slipped the gun inside.

It was still early afternoon, and Narcissa's kitchen was empty. Oona grabbed bread and cheese and dried meat and threw a few coins on the table. No note. She didn't have time, and they'd figure it out.

Did only crazy people go back? Well, then, she was crazy. Crazy with longing for Pace, and crazy with worry for him.

She wheeled the paint pony around and headed west toward Hall's Mill.

24

It took a week of hard riding to get back to
Hall's Mill. Oona had pushed the horse to
its limits until the night before. She'd
stopped early so they'd both be well rested
the next day. The paint walked into the town
with Oona on his back as if he owned the
place.

But something was very, very wrong. It
was more than the wrongness that had
brought Oona back. As Oona reined in the
paint pony in the Hall's Mill square, she
stared at babbling knots of women. The
shrill voices of some competed for attention, while others dabbed at their eyes with
their aprons. The mill stood silent, the
saloon darkened, and even fewer men were
about than on a normal weekday.

Oh, she didn't have time for this. *And
please don't let it be about Pace.* She dismounted, tied up the paint and ran over to
the nearest group. "What is it? What's hap-

pened?"

Women and children turned to her.

Mrs. Dale held her middle daughter, the formidable Rowena, with both arms. Rowena looked as though she'd been crying. Rowena never cried.

"They're gone," Julia Latham spoke, her narrow face alive with the gleam of good gossip. "Your sister-in-law. Two of the Dale girls, Zeb Wilkins, and the colored children."

"Jacksons." Oona wasn't in the mood for their casual cruelty.

"Jacksons," Julia amended with a blush. "They were carried off by some men earlier today. Rowena was the only one who escaped. Our men folk have gone to find 'em."

Lucy Foster's oldest son, Bobby Joe, hovered nearby. "Ma, Ma, can I go? I could catch up to them. I'm almost growed."

Lucy rounded on him with a smart slap to the cheek. "No, you ain't. You think I want to lose you too? Now git, and draw me some water for supper."

Oona had seen Lucy Foster suck snake venom out of this same boy's arm. Not much scared Lucy. But whoever this was, they'd even rattled her. Bobby Joe stomped off, and Oona tried to ignore her aching back. A week in the saddle, pushing the paint as hard as it would go, sleeping on moss, starting at every noise in the forest. Now this. "Do you know who took them?"

"Sadie at the hotel said it was Curtis." Lucy shook her head in wonder. "Took that to make her talk."

Victor Curtis. Curtis of the lingering gazes, the veiled suggestions. Yes, Caroline might appeal to him. But five little ones? Who could hate Caroline, gentle Caroline? Who could hate five children?

"But why the children?" Oona realized she was pleading.

"On account of she's been teaching the coloreds," Julia said. "Curtis don't like coloreds. He aims to punish her, and the kids too."

Curtis. At least that was starting to make sense. Curtis was behind the signs on the school door. Curtis was behind the burning of Michael's cabin. Curtis's prejudice was a passion even stronger than Caroline's appeal to him — and even uglier. And where was Pace? Was he with the rescue party? 'Twasn't like Pace to miss saving Caroline, and the five children. He loved Caroline like a sister, and his soft spot for kids was one of the things Oona loved about him. 'Twasn't like him at all, unless he hadn't had a choice.

Roy? Carl? Could she dare hope it wasn't them?

She turned away from the matrons, started to tie up the paint, and turned again at the clop of hooves.

Jenny crossed the square. She sat atop Rebel, with Pace's Prince on a lead. "Found him down by the mill, runnin' loose. Wherever Pace is, he ain't got a horse." She gave Oona a swift assessing look. "You're back. Good. You can help. Get on Prince, and I'll put your paint in the livery."

As if she'd seen Oona just that morning. Not much amazed Jenny, or even surprised her.

"My things —"

"Put the stuff you don't need in our old room. I'll be back in five minutes."

Oona threw her extra bags on her old bed. There were voices in the kitchen, a noise that sounded like sobbing, but she couldn't make herself go in there. Whatever it was, it would be fixed without her. Or not.

The room she'd shared with Jenny hadn't changed. The same two narrow beds, one rickety table, clothes-pegs on the walls. Her first home in the West. If she'd left this room to become Pace's bride, he'd still be in trouble, but at least they'd be facing it together. Instead, she'd left her little home to go back to Ireland. Oona took a deep breath and shut the door.

Jenny, already mounted, met her in the square. "Let's go. I'd be there now, but I had to take care of some stuff."

"Be where?"

"Wherever they took Caroline and the kids."

Oona swung onto Prince. She stuffed her fear down deep in the hiding place where she'd placed everything else that got in the way of survival. It would still be there when all of this stopped. It always was. "Jenny." Oona's teeth already chattered. "What will we do?"

"I got a plan."

They rode deeper into the forest, Jenny in the lead. Inexplicably, Jenny was humming.

Oona jogged along, confident that Pace's mount knew this terrain and trail. Could he lead her to his master? Oh, where was Pace? Mayhap he'd already learned about Caroline, Mrs. Wilkins, and the children, and had gone ahead to scout out a rescue. But without his horse?

She had never gone this deeply into the woods. She'd stayed in town, had everything she needed there. Now Jenny led her through places where the branches tangled overhead, where the trail disappeared for a few feet or broadened out for no perceptible reason. The dampness closed in around her, and a crow mocked her from a high branch. She smelled the mold under the leaves. The tall trees shut out the daylight. In this place, they always would.

Magical, mystical creatures, large beings that were spoken of by the local Indians in hushed tones, might lurk about. Oona knew about legends, her own Ireland had them too. Perhaps not the same monsters, but monsters none the less. This was a place where evil could flourish. But today's enemies were human. She knew that much. Oh, this place. But there was a raw beauty in the rich farmland and the towering forests. She wondered what the coast looked like. Maybe Pace would take her when this was over. She would never be afraid here with Pace at her side.

They stopped at a convergence of trails, and she reined Prince in as Jenny leaped lightly from Rebel's back.

"Git down. We got stuff to do." She rummaged in one of her saddlebags and tossed Oona a bundle of clothing. "Change into these pants and shirt. Plenty of trees for cover."

Oona clutched the garments to her chest. "I have never worn men's clothing."

Jenny shook her head, causing the wide-brimmed hat to fall down her back. "How was you planning to save Ireland? In a ball gown? Do it. Better'n a skirt for this job."

Oona's fingers tightened around the clothes. "You knew about that?"

Jenny snorted. "Next time it's my turn to clean our room, don't leave a crate of revolvers under your bed. Let's go."

Oona slipped behind a gnarled tree and shed her apron, dress, and chemise. The pants and shirt slid on like gloves. She tucked the revolver back in her holster before wadding up her clothes.

"Put 'em in the saddlebag," Jenny instructed. "You can change back when you're done. And here's a belt." She tossed Oona a gun belt and holster.

"I have one." Oona tossed it back and was rewarded by a very faint gleam of approval. She folded her arms across her chest. "Jenny, what are we doing?"

Jenny looked up from checking the stirrups on Rebel. "You're gonna find Pace, and I'm gonna help Michael get Caroline back." She said it as though it were the most reasonable thing in the world.

"I can't." Oona's hand flew to her throat. "Not alone."

Jenny's eyes narrowed. "You want to live in this country, you gotta do hard stuff."

She skimmed over the fact that Oona had never actually said she wanted to stay in Oregon Country. "And this is where we part ways. I'm goin' on to catch up with Mike's group, to wherever Victor Curtis's hideout is. I'm stayin' on the main road 'til it's time to turn off."

"Yes, but —"

"You're goin' to Barlow Camp. Ed at the bar said he saw one of the camp kids bring Pace a note this mornin'. Ed didn't think much about it, but then he got to wondering. Barlow people don't send kids on their errands. They like to drink. If they need somethin' in town, most likely one of the men comes in hisself. Ed thought it was odd, and he told me before he left with the posse."

"So —"

Jenny finished adjusting Rebel's tack. "So you're goin' after Pace. Start with Barlow Camp. Find the kid, find out who sent him to town."

"Wouldn't it be better if you —"

Jenny stopped fussing, looked full-on at Oona. "No. 'Cause what he wants is you. I'm gonna go help your fool brother like I always do. Can't do nothin' without me."

Of all the things she'd been forced to do in this country —

Jenny caught her hesitation and her blue gaze bored into Oona. "Oona Moriarty. Do you even realize what you have in Pace? Do you care? He's worth a dozen other men. He's worth a hundred Irelands. If I could've loved him I would've. But he loves you, and you can't see past a bunch of dead people."

"You do not understand."

"I understand plenty. I lost my family too. Some dead, some as good as dead. If you want to leave after this and go back to your precious Ireland, do it. But you're gonna try and save Pace first."

"How much do you know?"

"He's been spooked for a couple weeks. Seen something in the woods, and he's been skittish ever since. Why do you think he sent you away?"

Why, indeed? What force on God's green earth could make him encourage her to go back east, even to give her the money? How could she not have seen it, known it?

"Yeah, he's worried. Pace don't run, but he wanted you out of the way of whatever it is. I couldn't get him to say."

But Oona already knew.

Roy. Possibly Carl, if he was still alive.

"Iffen you love a person, you oughta know what scares them," Jenny said.

Oh, Oona knew. Too late, but she knew.

And it doubled her fear. "I cannot."

"Sure you can. 'Cause you'll be ridin' Rebel." Jenny swung onto Prince's back and grinned down at Oona. "Rebel's got a special talent even for him. He can track folks like a dog. When I was sick on the trail, he helped me find an Injun village where they took care of me. And when I got shot, he helped me catch up to Michael. He'll help ya find Pace."

For once in her life, Oona was out of words.

Jenny wheeled Prince around. "Take this road to the left. It'll lead you to the turnoff for Barlow Camp. They'll help ya from there." She dug her knees into Prince's flanks and was gone.

Oona wiped a bead of sweat from her forehead with the bandana Jenny had thoughtfully provided. She looked after her friend until Jenny's straight back disappeared for good. She stuffed her women's clothing in the saddlebag.

Could she do this? Jenny seemed to think so. But then Jenny could do anything — shoe a horse, run a hotel kitchen, deliver herself from a life of degradation. Jenny hadn't had her world defined by four hundred years of tradition. Jenny hadn't spent three years in a convent. Jenny hadn't —

Stop making excuses, Oona. She could hear Jenny's voice, crisp and slightly exasperated. And Jenny had let her — no, ordered her to take Rebel. Oona drew a deep breath, put her foot in the stirrup, and swung onto Rebel's back.

The stallion turned his head to look up at her, almost in a quizzical fashion, almost as if to ask, "Are we ready?"

She and Rebel.

Oona sighed and dug in her knees. "Let's go."

25

As Oona plodded toward Barlow Camp, she watched the sky. It was pewter gray, the air damper and cooler. Would she find Pace before the downpour? Was there still a Pace to find? The place was brooding, untouched, uncharted even on some maps. Easy to believe she was at the beginning of time — or the end. The trees formed a knotted canopy over her head. Some small animal skittered in the brush. She jumped, and then wiped her forehead with her flannel sleeve. If she was afraid, 'twas best to be afraid of something worth it. Pace. What had she done to him? Well, she hadn't done anything.

Roy Haskins was the do-er, or soon would be.

It was more what Oona hadn't done. Hadn't noticed the man she loved was troubled. Hadn't questioned his reversal on Ireland, the trip he'd been so dead set

270

against. Oh, she'd wondered, but not enough. Not enough to give up her daft dream or to give up dragging him into it. Had he meant it? Or was he as tired of her as she was of herself? If she couldn't find him in time, it didn't matter.

Here she was in men's clothing, walking a horse she could barely control through woods where anyone could hide anything. And jumping at every broken twig, every sigh of wind in the branches.

If the Novice Mistress could see her now, well, she'd never really approved of Oona. Oona'd given her good reason not to, about one good reason a day. More than once Sister had huffed, "Sister Oona, I do not know why you are here."

Oona could have told her, but it was better not to. Only Aunt Rose and Mother Superior knew the real reason she'd taken the veil. Every detail of that day was still clear after four years, down to the rumpled white shirtwaist, minus a button from young Hawthorne's groping, the dark skirt she'd worn, and her tumbled hair. Her fingers fumbling as she'd tried to make herself presentable while Michael stuffed straw under Hawthorne's head, in a vain effort to soak up the blood. Running before one of the other stable workers could happen by, pulling Tom in early from spring planting. He'd pay for it, but then, they all would. No time to grab her things, no time to say goodbye to Ma. Tom harnessed the faster of their plow horses, Oona rode pillion behind him to Dublin.

Walking up the steps of the convent, ringing a bell that echoed deep within. She'd waited in a barren parlor for Aunt Rose, now Sister Mary Boniface, whom they hadn't seen since childhood. Tom pulled their aunt aside, speaking to her in low tones, and Oona knew he'd reached the reason for their visit when the nun's work-worn hands flew to her thin cheeks.

Oona and Tom had waited for an hour in that parlor, under grim portraits of Superiors past, while Sister Boniface sought her superior. At last, the Reverend Mother Mary Gonzaga came to greet them. There was more murmured conversation, and then they'd led Oona inside to a rabbit warren of rooms scented with lemon furniture polish and incense. She hadn't dared look back at Tom; if she had, she'd known she would bolt. Most girls underwent a lengthy application process. But Oona was a postulant, in short veil and simple black dress, before bedtime.

Though the order wasn't cloistered, postulants and novices rarely left the Mother House. Oona had stayed out of Hawthorne's powerful reach, and Michael had carried her guilt on his big shoulders to the New World.

Oona had tried her best, learning the Benedictine offices, chanting 'til her lips were numb, going without sleep to attend Matins and Lauds in the middle of the night. Sleep. It was the first thing she'd done when she got out, using part of her precious five pounds to rent a room in a boarding-house. She'd slept for eighteen hours, she'd figured out later. But when she woke, what was there was still there. And what was gone, was gone.

Kevin. She let herself think about him as she plodded through a landscape he could never have imagined, let alone visited. She listened in her mind to his laughter one more time, relived his kisses. She mused on his curly blond hair, the quick grin and quick wit, the strong arms that held her. Why couldn't he have waited, instead of taking on the English in one more doomed battle? Well, what had he had to wait for? A fiancé who'd disappeared from the known world.

He would have come to the cottage, banging on the door, demanding, after too many excuses, to know where she'd gone. Michael would have been gone by then. Poor Tomeen, who had to concoct a story. Tom hated lying. What had he come up with, that she was away helping a sick relative? In their village, that was code for a girl in trouble. Kevin must have been devastated, knowing the baby couldn't possibly have been his, except there was no baby. And in a week, it hadn't mattered. The Moriartys were gone, relieved of their tenancy, allowed only what they could wear or carry. The cottage was demolished, the Moriartys banished from the village.

Oona's hands slackened on the reins.

Well, no wonder.

No wonder Kevin had thrown himself into the Valley of the Shadow, joined the rebels. He'd planned a raid on one of the manor houses. He'd died for Ireland, that's what he'd done. As pointless as . . . as what she was planning. Go to Ireland and die trying to make a difference. For what?

And where had God been in all of this? Why had He allowed her to become attacked? Why had He allowed her and young Hawthorne to be in the barn on the same day? And why had hot-tempered Michael been the one to intercept them? Where had God been in the whole tangled history of her people? There was no reason to think He'd help her now. Someone else should be rescuing Pace, someone who knew how.

Pace.

If it weren't for Ireland and England, she never would have known of his existence. She'd have lived out her life in an Irish village as the blacksmith's wife, or more likely, his widow. A tidy life bound by tradition like the hedgerows that defined their fields, and safe as long as one kept on the right side of the English. If only she could pour her life back into that mold.

One of her first chores had been gathering the eggs. She'd been but three or four, puffed up with pride as she'd crossed the chicken yard with her brimming basket. She'd walked too fast when she saw Ma, and one of the speckled brown ovals had slipped from the basket to the packed earth. She'd knelt in the dirt, crying as her stubby fingers tried to scoop the yolk back into the shell until she felt Ma's hand on her shoulder. "Oona, love, don't. Once it's spilled, sure, and you can never get it back in. Just look at all the lovely eggs you've kept!"

Oona had crossed America, seen the West, and loved a western man. Could she ever fit back into village life? Mayhap, no, even if there was a village that wanted her.

She'd done her best not to listen to Caroline's speech, but enough had slipped through. Caroline had said, " 'You meant it for evil but God meant it for good.' "

Oona pulled on the reins, and though she could feel his coiled tension, Rebel obeyed.

"You meant it for evil."

"God meant it for good."

Not Hawthorne, nothing could justify an attempt at rape. But God had known about it from the beginning of time. That's why He was God. He had given man free will. He had a pretty good idea of what man would do with it.

She shivered. *Lord . . . Sir . . . Father.* Had it all been leading up to this moment, the moment she would rescue Pace Williams?

Jenny could have saved him, or Michael.

Were they here by accident?

No. No more than she was.

The sweep of Creation, from forbidden fruit to three crosses. Stories she'd listened to in parish school, at Mass, at home by the fire. How sin entered the world through one man, and was gloriously, permanently atoned for by Another.

And if someone missed a cue, it didn't matter. He did it anyway. The God of the universe knew where she was on a borrowed stallion in the Oregon Country woods, and

He knew what would happen and why.

She lifted her face to the cloudy sky. *Father — dear Lord — 'tis sorry I am for doubting You. I'll stay as long as You want me to. I'll be what You want me to be. And if I don't go back, I'll pray for Ireland the rest of my life.* She clucked to Rebel, and he began to move again, a leisurely walk, all even he could manage in this narrow valley. She bowed her head for just a second. *And Father, please help me find Pace.*

26

Was that an ant marching across Pace's shirt? No, it was a whole line of 'em. Some were getting under his clothes; he could feel them. He strained to move his hand to brush them off, but the rope held it fast. Better the ants than the vultures that would come later. Roy and Carl didn't seem the type to go in for decent burials.

He started at every sound from the woods. Were they back? Pace tried to find a comfortable position, as comfortable as a man could get when he was chained across a rock. The exposed parts of his flesh were pink from the cold and his limbs ached from stiffness.

It wasn't the pain he dreaded, leastways not much. In nineteen years of farmin', cowboyin', loggin' and working the wagon train, plus some less legitimate pursuits, he'd broken every bone there was; been shot with white men's bullets, and red men's arrows; felt the slice of a yellow man's knife. He could take what Roy threw at him until he passed out or died.

But they wouldn't make it that easy.

He strained at his ropes but they didn't move, and the effort cut deep into his flesh. He sank back to the rock, tried again, and fell back exhausted. He had to get to the kid who'd brought the note to the saloon. Couldn't let Roy or Carl kill the boy to keep anyone from knowing what happened. Any woman they approached, too, but one they would seek would probably come willingly if Roy paid her enough. Still, it was Roy, and Pace wouldn't wish him on any woman.

Would he live to see Oona again? If he did, he'd go with her on her fool journey. Better to die together than to die alone.

But he wouldn't die, wouldn't let evil win this time. Bernadette had been one time too many. He had to live. Had to save the boy and whatever woman Roy had managed to find. He twisted his head, tried to reach the rope to bite through it, but it was too far away. Roy and Carl were professionals; he'd give them that. And they knew how to drive in all the knives, not just the physical ones.

Had anyone ever loved him? Not until Bernadette, and until Oona, not after.

Ma certainly hadn't, but she'd borne his

birth with a fair amount of goodwill. He was a toy, an amusement. She fed and clothed him when she remembered, and dragged him out to show her customers in the river town, the mining town, the logging town. "Ugly little monkey, but smart as a whip," she'd boasted. Until he was three, she'd left him with a neighbor while she took care of business. After that, he was old enough to sit on the steps of whatever shack or brothel they lived in until she was done.

He called the men "Uncle." Uncle Ray, Uncle Rufus, Uncle Jimmy. They pretty much left him alone, 'cept for the occasional peppermint stick, until Uncle Walter came on the scene and wanted him gone. And his Ma dumped him as easily as that.

Roy and Carl were right. No one had ever loved him. He'd been a number at the orphanage, "Boy" to everyone else. He'd changed his name when he took to the road, but they'd found him anyway.

So cold . . .

What had it all been worth, anyway? Oona'd probably forgotten him. He would if he were her. The boy nobody wanted. He wasn't good enough for Oona. Why hadn't she seen it? Even his parents hadn't wanted him. Oona would move on, should move on. Would Mike be able to reach her to tell her what had happened? That Pace was dead? Or would he fade from her life as he had from so many lives? Perhaps he'd be another story to be told in that singsong, storytelling voice. "There was a man I knew one time, in the West . . ."

A white-tailed deer, the gentlest of animals, came up to him, sniffed him, cautiously licked his face.

And for the first time in nineteen years, Pace cried.

His throat was parched. He'd been thirsty before, but never with his hands and feet bound. Maybe he'd die this way. No, he wouldn't be that lucky. Roy and Carl would be back before thirst claimed him. He turned his head and his tears trickled on to the flat rock. *Sure wished I could've saved that kid. And said good-bye to Oona. Wouldn't mind dyin' then. Not as much, anyway.*

Son.

The deer lowered herself to the ground behind him, a witness to whatever was happening. The words weren't out loud, more of a feeling, but Pace twisted his head anyway. It was a man's voice. *Son?* He'd had even less of a father than he'd had of a ma.

"Ain't . . . nobody's . . . son," he rasped.

Son.

A warmth coursed through him. He wanted to bow, to prostrate himself, but he could only move his head. So this was how it happened. He was dying. No Roy, no Carl — that was good — but no Oona either.

"Sir." Was this the part where Pace was supposed to apologize? Where was a good place to start?

Before you were in the womb, I knew you.

He swallowed. "Is that in Your Bible, Sir?"

It is. And behold, I have loved you with an everlasting love.

He didn't even believe in God. Did he? Guess he did now.

"Sir, I'm awful sorry . . . sorry for the way I've lived." His throat was dry, too dry to talk, and his lips were beginning to blister. Well, God could hear thoughts, couldn't He? *I want to be forgiven. I want what Mike has, an' Caroline — even if I die tonight. Especially if I die tonight.*

You are My son. You are My son for all eternity, Paul Walker.

Paul Walker. The name he'd given up when he'd started his wanderings. The name Aggie, his mother, inadequate as she was, had bestowed on him. *I have a Father. And I have a name. My name is Paul.*

The doe unfolded herself and loped back into the woods.

And as the Presence receded, a gentle spring rain began to fall.

Pace opened his mouth like a baby bird.

27

It took a lot to make Hall's Mill look good, but Oona guessed Barlow Camp could do it. She reined Rebel to a stop. The logging camp huddled under a stand of ancient fir trees. The few buildings were scattered, like forgotten children's blocks, pointing any which way. Smoke curled from the chimney of the largest building, most likely the cook shack, but the other cabins were dark.

In the center of the clearing, a man, who looked as though he'd been carved from one of the trees, loaded logs from a travois to a wagon. A young boy, eleven? thirteen? helped him. The boy's hair was shaggy, his pants an inch too short, and he wore no coat despite the brewing clouds.

Oona tried to remember if she'd seen the youth around Hall's Mill. Had he been in Caroline's school? "A good afternoon to you," she called.

The man stopped stacking and looked at

her with dull eyes. "Whaddya want?"

"I am looking for Mr. Pace Williams, the courier. I have a — a message for him." Her message was that she wanted Pace to live, that they could start over somewhere.

The man spat on the ground. "Ain't seen 'im."

Pace had rescued and added to this boy's birthday money. Maybe the child could help. "Do you happen to remember Mr. Williams? Has he been through here today?"

She'd been an older sister most of her life, and she could read children.

Fear. Bone-deep fear.

His name was Lucas. She remembered it now. Oona dismounted, keeping a firm hand on Rebel, and moved closer to the child. "Lucas, Mr. Williams may be in danger. I need to help him, and you can, too. Please tell me what you know."

The boy cut his gaze to the older man. "Uncle Enos?"

The man spat again. "Up to you."

Lucas coughed. Really, the child shouldn't be out in this damp without a coat. She doubted he even had one. When she got back to town, she'd talk to some of her customers, maybe gather some used clothing for the Barlow kids.

He was tall for his age, with brown hair

285

and eyes and narrow features. He had the hollow cheeks of a person who hadn't had much to eat. She knew what that looked like, too. He avoided looking at her. Was it shame for his poverty or shame for what he knew?

Oona touched the boy's threadbare sleeve. How long would this take? "Do you know where he is?" *Please, Lucas.* She held her breath.

Lucas looked at the ground. "He's with Mr. Roy and Mr. Carl."

Roy and Carl. She'd hoped with everything in her that she'd been wrong. Why did she have to be right this time? Oona's fingers clenched on the reins. With her sister-in-law and five children in the hands of madmen, she'd thought this day couldn't get any worse. Well, it just had. How had Roy gotten free? How had they found Pace? Well, this wasn't the time to ask why. It wasn't the time to ask anything, really. She had to get to Pace. "You have to help me find them."

The fear in the boy's eyes flared into panic. "No, ma'am. I done my part. I'm a'scared of them. Mr. Carl, he looks like he wants to kill me. An' Mr. Roy said they'd hurt me iffen I told."

Oona looked up at the blackening sky. Was

that a drop of rain? Precious minutes were being lost. Was Pace already dead? No, those two would drag it out and enjoy it. "I won't tell. If you show me where their camp is, I'll pretend I found it on my own."

"No." The boy was terrified.

The uncle took a plug of tobacco out of his cheek. "Williams, he's been decent to us. Go with the woman, Lucas. Then git back here and help me with the logs."

Whatever he saw in his uncle's face seemed to scare Lucas almost as much as Carl and Roy. At a gesture from Oona, he clambered up behind her.

"Hold me close, Lucas, so you don't fall off." She hoped he'd absorb some of her bodily warmth. He snuggled close, his body trembling, from fear or the cold, she didn't know.

They retraced her steps to the main trail and went a half mile back toward town, the boy giving directions in a dull voice and volunteering nothing else. Maybe conversation would keep her mind off what surely lay ahead. "Did you go to the school when they had it?"

"No'm. Uncle Enos needed me in the woods. I can read some, learned it afore we come here."

Oona's mind raced ahead. Anything to get

her thoughts off Pace. Maybe she could get this child a job in town. Maybe Molly could use a boy at the hotel. Yes. Molly was good at taking in strays. She'd taken Sadie, hadn't she? And Oona. Room and board, decent clothing, a chance at school if it opened up again. He was afraid of Roy and Carl, rightly so. *God, don't let them hurt or kill him. He's just a boy.*

The mountains closed in around them, the trail that was barely there narrowed. Rebel picked his way along the stony path.

The boy was silent for a good half hour, answering her questions in monosyllables. "Their camp's about a mile in, over that little rise," he said at last.

"Splendid. Thank you, Lucas. You can go now."

Lucas gave a little sigh. "No, ma'am. I can't."

And she felt the butt of a revolver in her back.

"You little, you're not . . ."

"Roy figgered you'd be back. He said they wouldn't kill me if I delivered you. Said they'd pay me, too," Lucas's voice wobbled.

"And you believed them?"

"Keep ridin', lady." His changing voice ended on a creaky note.

Held hostage by a child. A child in the

pay of Pace's oldest enemies.

She searched her own arsenal and pulled out her big-sister voice. "You should be ashamed of yourself."

"Keep ridin', lady. And shut up. I ain't changin' my mind."

Lord, show me what to do. Please, Lord. For Pace. And for Lucas. She'd seen Jenny do the trick once, just showing off. Would Rebel cooperate for Oona? She gave a sharp tug on the bit, whispered "Up, boy!"

Rebel reared up on two powerful legs.

Oona wasn't Jenny and neither was Lucas. They both lost their balance, and both tumbled to the earth. She landed hard, but there was no time to worry about bumps and bruises.

The gun flew from the boy's hand and landed under a scrub. Lucas stood poised, his fists raised, his legs slightly apart as he inched toward it. "Don't touch it, lady."

Well, girls didn't fight that way, especially Irish girls with five brothers. She didn't even need a gun for this one. Oona stretched out one long leg, tripped the boy, and sent him tumbling. She had her belt off before he could gain purchase. She pushed down when he tried to get up and put one knee on his back. Using her bandana, she fastened his hands behind him. She dragged him to a small fir tree, propped him against the trunk and secured him with her belt.

She retrieved Lucas's gun and tucked it in her waistband. Well, that made two. She stopped to catch her breath. "Lucas, you'll be fine there for a while. I'm goin' on, so I am, and we'll talk on my way back. I'll see about getting you a job in town. You don't deserve it, faith, nobody ever deserved it less, but I can't have you pulling this kind of thing again. And if you're not desperate, you won't."

Lucas strained at his makeshift bonds. "I'll get loose, ya know."

"I know you will, eventually. But you won't 'til I'm well on my way. And I've got the horse and the gun." She mounted Rebel again and looked down at the wretched boy. "We'll talk when I get back."

And however difficult the conversation turned out to be, it had to be easier than rescuing Pace from two madmen.

28

As Oona drew even deeper into the woods, she sat up straight and forgot about being tired. She was near him now. She could sense it. The rain dripped into her collar and onto Rebel's mane. It was smart of Jenny to wear that broad-brimmed hat. Oona would have to pick one up for herself. In this country, she'd need something like that. Her country now, for better or worse.

Rebel flicked the rain off and plunged ahead. Did he sense it too? That Pace was near?

But if he was, so were Roy and Carl.

What would she say? What would she do? She'd outwitted Lucas, but these were no twelve-year-old boys. Nothing in her life had prepared her for this, not Hawthorne, not the western journey, and certainly not the convent. She didn't think anything could have prepared her. And what would she say to Pace after? If there was an after.

The trail, now barely a rutted path, ended abruptly at a cliff. Water rushed over the rocks below. She calculated she was upstream, near the source of the river that carried logs to Hall's Mill. Rain darkened the water and the rocks under it. Everything was gray where it wasn't black.

Rebel pushed through a break in the trees and they came out into a small clearing.

Stubby grass covered the ground and shone with wetness. Gear and supplies were strewn about, and a cooking fire looked damp and long-dead. The rest of the landscape was bare save for a large flat rock, worn smooth by years of snow and rain.

Oona choked back a sob. That couldn't be Pace — that pale form spread across the stone, his hair matted with rain, his tanned arms stretched against the slick gray rock.

But it was. She leaped from Rebel before he'd come to a full stop. She ran to Pace, knelt in the wet grass and ran an experimental hand across his cold cheek.

This was where she needed to be.

He had to be dreaming. Or dead. Was that Oona coming toward him, in Jenny's clothes and on Jenny's horse? If this was death, it could be worse. But he'd kind of expected to see God too.

Oona dismounted and ran to him, slipping in the mud. She cradled his cheek with one hand as she leaned over him. "Pace. Oh, Pace. What is it they've done to you?"

"I'm all right." *Now.* He drank in the sight of her, the blue eyes dark with worry, the black braid she flipped over her shoulder with impatience. She had mud on one cheek. No, he wasn't dead. His Oona would have insisted on a clean face in Heaven. Time enough later to ask why she'd come back.

Oona set to work on the rope coils, tearing at the one over his left arm.

He could have told her it wouldn't do any good.

"The shaft goes clear into the rock. They're professionals." He jerked his head toward their stuff. "There's gear over there. See what you can find."

He twisted his head enough to watch Oona rummage through the stuff. He didn't want to let her out of his sight for a minute. She flung their possessions across the wet grass, good for her, and returned with a penknife and a canteen of water. She tipped the canteen into his mouth, and he drank deeply and felt his energy return. *Thank You, Sir.* He couldn't bow his head, but God knew.

"The knife looks sharp enough," Oona murmured.

She looked away from his half-naked form and began to saw at the coiled rope. Her face was intent, her lips a thin line; she'd give this everything she had. The first one fell away. He lifted an experimental hand. Numb, but free. As she hacked away at his other bonds he said, "Oona."

She shot a questioning gaze from those deep blue eyes.

"When you cut me loose, make it look like you didn't. 'S'what Caroline did in the Blue Mountains. Nobody knew she was free, and she saved the day for everyone."

"Caroline?" Oona rocked back on her booted heels.

"Yeah." She had things to learn about her sister-in-law, but he wasn't the one to teach her. "If they're surprised, it will throw 'em off."

Oona cast an uneasy look at the trail. "We can run. We can escape. I've got Rebel —"

"They might hurt someone else. Might bring someone with them. And I'm not runnin' no more. It ends here."

"But you're cold and wet."

She was fussin' over him, and he liked it. But Roy and Carl had to be stopped. For the woman Roy went to find today, for Bernadette and Pace's childhood, for the nuns. Yeah, it ended here.

"I can stand it a little longer." Cold and wet were the least of his worries. "Now. Tell me how you got here." Pace lifted himself on one elbow.

Oona crouched at his side, and he breathed in her scent of soap and rain.

"I'm not really sure. Reverend Whitman told me about a boy who'd brought a message to you, asked me if he'd reached you, and I just knew I had to come back. I didn't remember a boy coming to town, and I had a bad feeling. I thought about . . . about . . . what you told me, and wondered if the boy, if there was a boy, was killed after he delivered the message. When I got to Hall's Mill, Jenny loaned me Rebel, said he'd find you. She went off on Prince, because she had to help Michael rescue Caroline."

"What happened to Caroline?" Pace was having a hard time following her logic.

"I'm not sure. But 'tis nasty, whatever it is. So Jenny sent me after you. Lucas, you remember him, the boy you gave birthday money to. I thought he would help me. But he pulled a gun on me, and I trussed him like a chicken."

He wouldn't expect anything less of her. "Still got the gun?" He had no idea what

295

was going on from her garbled story, but having a weapon seemed to be a good idea.

"I've got two. Mine and Lucas's. You should take one."

She reached for her holster.

They both froze as they heard a rustling in the brush.

29

Roy's voice, indecently cheerful, preceded him into the clearing. Pace would know that voice anywhere, even coarsened with age. He'd know it if he was blindfolded in the Sahara Desert.

"Well, we couldn't find any pleasure. Lucas done scampered. Maybe tomorrow. Not sure if we should feed you to keep you alive, or . . ." Roy skidded to a stop. His small eye, the good one, raked Oona from head to toe. "Looky here, Carl. We got ourselves some fresh meat. The princess done come back. An' don't she look like Bernadette?"

Carl smirked. "She do, Roy. She sure do."

"This could be interestin'." He moved toward Oona, who still crouched beside Pace, and yanked her to her feet. She struggled in arms that gripped her like a vise. She spat at him, and Roy gave her a quick slap to the cheek, as though he was swatting a fly.

With everything that was in him, Pace wanted to defend her. But he forced his breathing to evenness. Not yet. Wait until they were off guard. Roy and Carl could do much worse than a slap.

"We'll have a little fun an' he can watch," Roy said. "Be like old times, hey?"

"Yeah." Carl squatted beside Pace, wrenched Pace's head so he could watch Oona struggle.

Roy's meaty fingers fumbled with the buttons on Oona's shirt. His other arm held her like iron, and she squirmed in his grip. Her boots slipped in the mud and Roy yanked her upright. She recoiled at the closeness, most likely at his breath. Pace would've, too.

"That's good, girlie. I like a good fight. Hey, you a virgin?"

"You. Will. Not. Touch. Me."

No, he wouldn't. It was time. Pace heaved himself up from the stone, throwing Carl backward into the wet grass. He charged Roy like a bull, driving his head into the older man's stomach. Roy's eyes widened, and in the moment of surprise, Pace shoved Oona away.

"Run!"

He knew all along that she wouldn't.

Her black hair was matted to her head, her shirt half-open to reveal a white camisole. Rain and tears streaked Oona's face. But she pulled out the revolver Jenny had given her and trained it on Pace and Roy.

"Let him go, Roy, or whatever your name is. Or I'll shoot."

"Ya might miss. Might hurt your sweetheart," Roy grunted.

"Take the chance, Oona," Pace yelled.

But she wavered at the last second, and Carl came up behind and tripped her into the wet grass. Flat on her back, she trained the gun on Carl as he straddled her.

"Can you even shoot?" Carl jeered.

"I will blow your brains out if your friend doesn't let Mr. Williams go."

Only someone who knew her well, or even loved her, could pick up on the quaver under the steeliness.

Carl twisted his head. "Roy?"

Roy shrugged, and tightened his grip on Pace. "You're on your own, boy. I done waited too long for this."

But Oona didn't fire.

This was it. Oona swallowed. Sure, and they could hear her heart pounding back in Hall's Mill. Could she take a life, even one as miserable as this Carl's? He hadn't killed

Bernadette. Done just about everything else, but he wasn't the main villain here. Maybe she could knock Carl out. Or — or something.

At least Lucas had gotten away from Roy and Carl. She'd deal with that boy when this was over. Oona slammed the gun into the side of Carl's head, and he fell away. She scrambled to her feet, raised her gun again in trembling hands and pointed it at Roy. "As I was saying . . ."

Carl grabbed her from behind, wrapping his long arms around her chest, pinning the arm that held the gun. With her left hand, she scrabbled for Jenny's extra gun from her holster and sent it flying through the air. "Pace!"

He managed to throw Roy off, caught it with one hand, backed off, and pointed it at his oldest enemy.

Carl held Oona, almost cutting off her breath.

Pace signaled her with his eyes. *Don't do anything.*

How could she not?

Behind them Rebel fussed and snorted, pawing the damp ground.

If Oona were free, she could ride away. But she wouldn't. Not without Pace.

And Roy was laughing, his head thrown

back, exposing a row of stumpy teeth. Laughing at Pace. "You think I care? You're nobody, boy. Still."

"Ain't your place to judge."

Roy moved, slipped a little in the grass, slid into Pace just enough to knock him down. Pace's revolver streaked across the wet grass.

Roy grabbed it and pointed it at Oona and Carl. "I took something you loved from you once, boy. I'll teach you a lesson and do it again. My aim's as good as it ever was, 'spite of only one eye."

"Not her. Please."

"Don't beg," Oona called to him. "They're not worth it." She shifted in Carl's grip, becoming a dead weight.

The bullet Roy meant for Oona went into Carl. A red stain bloomed on Carl's shirt, and his hold on her loosened as he fell to the ground.

Roy shrugged. "Small loss. I was gonna get rid of him anyway. Slowed me down too much."

Pace, nearly blind with fury and the need to save Oona, tackled Roy and brought him down. Strength he didn't even know he had surged as he straddled the big man. Roy thrashed and clawed at his face, trying to drive his other fist into Pace's stomach. The blow glanced off his body, but Pace punched him back. Roy went still as his eyes rolled back into his head. Pace yanked at the belt from Roy's dungarees, grimly satisfied as it slid out in seconds, and bound the man's hands.

Roy, senses returning, but still a little groggy from Pace's punch, spat in his face. Pace didn't bother to wipe it off. Kneeling on Roy's chest, he reached for the ropes on the ground that had bound him. With a quick wrap and a tight knot, he hobbled Roy's feet.

Roy flopped about like a fresh-caught fish. Funny, at least for Pace, to see him helpless. It was the last word one would ever think to hear in connection with Roy Haskins.

"Whyn't you just kill me? That's what you want."

Did he? On the trail he'd had to mediate disputes, hundreds of them. He'd been the only law the travelers had. He'd stopped people from killing each other on a regular basis. But had any of the emigrants had a Roy in their lives? This man had killed the only person in Pace's childhood who was even close to a mother, had propelled a young boy on the journey that made him a man too fast. Pace had looked for that familiar stocky silhouette in every river town and lumber camp. He'd wondered what he'd do if Roy found him. Wondered what he'd do if he'd found Roy.

He could end it here, bring the outcome he'd dreamed about to the person he'd dreaded and feared for nineteen years. Get revenge for Bernadette — and himself. Revenge on the man who had robbed him of what little childhood he'd had left. He picked up one of the revolvers. It felt cold and smooth in his hands. Roy was a monster. It would do the world a favor if Pace put him down now. But what would that make Pace?

Roy had set him on the journey that had brought him to Oona. Whatever else he'd done, whatever else he'd been, there was that.

Did God's mercy extend to Roy too? As it had to Pace?

Could Pace do this?

No.

Was it out of his hands?

Yes.

Pace rocked back on his heels. "Ain't gonna kill you, Haskins. I been around a while, and I never killed a man I didn't have to. Ain't startin' now. There's no law in

303

Hall's Mill, so I'm takin' you to the authorities in Oregon City."

He wasn't prepared for Roy's shake of the head, the closing of his one good eye, the violent trembling. "No. No jail."

"Not my decision," Pace said. "That'd be up to the territorial authorities."

"You could shoot me. Got no reason not to."

Oona's hand was warm on Pace's shoulder. He reached up and covered it with his own. He had everything he needed. Revenge was a luxury. "Don't want to do that, Haskins."

"Then I'll kill myself," He reached for the gun with his bound hands.

Pace grabbed the revolver, not that he needed it now, and knelt beside Roy. "I didn't mean for it to end like this, Haskins. I just . . . why couldn't you leave me alone?"

"I can't go to jail again." Roy strained against his bonds. "You don't know what it's like to be locked up."

Didn't Pace? Until today, he'd never known what it was like to be free.

The one good eye took on a wild look. "Never feel the fresh air, 'cept when they got you breakin' rock. Felt the whip on my back, though. Fought for my life ever' day for eighteen years. Fought the other prisoners, fought the guards. Ain't goin' back."

"We'll let the judge decide that. We're taking you to justice, Haskins. Not taking justice on ourselves."

Did he still hate Roy? Could anyone hate this helpless wreck of a man? No. He hated what Roy had done. He'd see that no one else suffered at Roy's hands. But hate? No. Trial or no, this was where it ended for Pace.

Roy lunged to his feet, throwing Pace back with the impact.

As Pace rolled on the ground, Roy moved in, kicking him in the stomach. Pace writhed and curled up, completely winded.

Oona rushed to him, dropping to her knees, but her right hand held the gun steady on Roy.

Roy stared at her and the belt fell away from his hands. He'd used the same trick Caroline used in the Blue Mountains, hiding the fact she was free from her bonds.

Pace struggled to breathe, to tell Oona to watch out, but a bare whistling breath was all he could manage.

Instead of rushing Oona, Roy reached down, pulled the knot loose from his ankles. "She never loved me. She loved you three boys." He ran off into the woods.

The afternoon was silent, the sky darkening into early evening. A hawk swooped low.

Twigs broke and a slim, gray hare ran out of the trees.

Pace struggled for air, panic radiating through his entire body. He stilled, clawing for control.

"We should bring him back. He has to face what he's done." Oona looked at Pace.

"Let him go. He won't get far." Pace wheezed the words out.

Oona clutched his arm. "Pace, 'tis the cliff. I saw it on the way in."

Pace was finally able to suck in a deep breath. He got to his feet, still a little wobbly, but pushed his weakness aside. His shambling run towards the woods was slower than Oona's. She took off ahead of him.

"Haskins!" he called, but his voice was too hoarse. *Dear God, let them get there in time.*

In the afternoon stillness, the splashing sound of something hit the water.

They ran to the edge of the cliff.

Roy's body looked like a rag doll being tossed about in the churning water. His head smacked into a floating log and even from this distance, Pace could see the blood before it was washed away. Roy's body sagged even more and then he went under. Pace waited, staring this way and that, trying to spot Roy. Nothing. He looked past the log, down river. Roy was gone.

Pace sagged against Oona. He was suddenly more tired than he'd been all day. "He's gone. I didn't want — I didn't think —"

Oona hung on to him for dear life. "I know you didn't. Are you all right?"

"Been better." Roy's skills hadn't rusted in prison. Pace was winded from that kick in the stomach. He had a shiner forming. His nose was probably broken, and he had at least two broken fingers. All would mend.

Oona hugged him once more, hard, before she stood back and appraised him. "Sure, and you need to get warm. Where did they put your coat? It's probably damp, but better than nothing."

"Not yet." Pace let her support him as they walked toward Rebel, now grazing peacefully. "Somebody's got to find Roy and bury the other poor devil." Compassion, at last, for Roy and Carl. What a day this had turned out to be.

"Not you." Oona's voice was firm, the quaver gone. "I don't want you touching them. I'll send someone out from the village. We are going home."

While he painfully shrugged into his damp coat, Oona collected the three revolvers and

307

covered the dead man with a blanket she found in their camp. She swung up on Rebel, and Pace mounted behind her. All his bones ached. A fire would be good, and a cup of coffee.

Oona rode with her back straight as Rebel picked his way down the path.

She had come back. To this. For this. For him. "Oona, honey," he said, trying out the word. He had never used it with any living being. "I'll go to Ireland with you. It don't matter anymore."

She half-turned, the reins loose in her hands. "I don't know as you'll have time, Mr. Williams. You've got to help tame this land, and stake your claim, and build a big, two-story log house for your crazy Irish wife so she can fill it with crazy, half-Irish children."

Pace wrapped his arms around her waist. "Sounds good."

It was the most reasonable thing he'd heard all day.

They saw the rooftops of Hall's Mill and the curling smoke of a few supper fires. As they descended the last hill, a party of horsemen met them from a converging trail.

Joe Foster was holding Elijah Jackson as firmly as he'd hold one of his own sons.

Moses was on a borrowed horse with little Deborah huddled in his arms. A group of men, their faces blackened by smoke, were holding the other children. And Michael had Caroline riding in front of him, cradled in his arms. Her brother sat astride, with all the fierceness gone out of him, a drained Michael, and an even more exhausted Caroline.

Oona reined Rebel to a stop. "What happened, Michael?"

He wiped his forehead and left a blackened smear. "Curtis didn't like the school. Didn't like the coloreds to begin with. Didn't want them in town. So he kidnapped Caroline and the children, and made his threat. He was going to burn down a shack, with them in it unless the Jacksons agreed to leave Hall's Mill."

"I would have done it," Moses said, his voice soft with weariness. "If it would save Miss Caroline and those kids, I would have left. But the other men stood behind me, and they got Miss Caroline and the kids out."

"Caroline." Oona knotted her hands in front of her. Brave Caroline, who would risk her life for her students. All of them. How else had Oona underestimated her? "Are you all right?"

"I am." Her sister-in-law sent Oona a look as fierce and brave as any Irish queen. "I'm fine, the baby's fine, and the children are fine."

"Victor?" Pace's voice came from behind her, his breath warm on her neck. The Pace she'd almost lost. *Thank You, Lord, for making me come back. Even if I didn't know it was You at the time.*

Michael exchanged glances with Joe Foster and Ned Wilkins. "Tucker Creek needs a new boss," was all he needed to say.

30

Oona knocked lightly on Pace's door. She heard a growled "C'mon in. It's open. If it's Jenny, I don't need no more food," Pace tacked on.

A fire burned in the grate with Jenny's food offerings spread on an overturned barrel.

Pace, wrapped in wool blankets, sat on his pallet. And didn't his face light up when he saw her?

She was wearing skirts again and lowered gently to his side. "How are you?"

"Better. Thanks. Nothin' that won't heal. Nothin' I haven't faced before. Mostly, I took a chill. Caroline's been fussin' over me, and Jenny's been in and out. I think she's brought me every bit of food in the hotel kitchen."

"Good. Molly's been fussing over me. I got here as soon as I could."

"I ain't goin' anywhere. Not without you,

anyways."

His face seemed thinner, the black eye fading to green. She laced her fingers through his, and they were quiet for several minutes. The quiet of people who would talk when they were ready, because they had the time.

"So. What's the news in town?"

"Oh, Pace. Everything's changed."

"Do tell." His expression went on alert, interested in anything she had to say.

"Well, everyone's making amends to the Jacksons. Annie Two Stars even offered Moses the store. She wants to go back up to Canada for a while. He'd be a full manager, not a clerk. With a salary."

"That could work."

"It could. It could also be a big risk." All they needed was a new crop of settlers who didn't want a colored man running a store.

"Moses will do the right thing. What else?"

"Oh, Pace. Ed Petersen is dead."

He sat straighter. "What happened?"

"When Curtis set fire to the cabin, he ran inside and held up the beam so the others could get out. But he couldn't get out himself. Caroline looked back and she said he looked like a Norse god, holding up that roof, surrounded by fire. He never made it out." Oona had tears in her eyes.

"He was a good man."

"Yes," she whispered.

Until the end, none of them had realized how good.

"They . . . they found Roy's body. Some loggers down river fished him out and buried him."

"I guess that's good. At least we know he's truly dead." It was all Pace could think of to say about the man who'd dogged him for years. His own burden had lifted on the rock, and now all he could do was wonder if Roy had time in the river to call out to God.

They sat on, holding each other, content with being together.

Oona remembered what it had taken to get them here. Faith, and would she ever forget it? "Something happened to me on the trail," she said at last.

"Yeah? Besides everything else?" He didn't move, but his expression snapped into alertness again.

"Yes. I was moping and worrying about how I would manage, and . . . and God was there." She waited. Would he laugh or shrug it off? Would he belittle what she'd learned and become?

But Pace nodded in the thoughtful way she loved.

"He done that to me, too. When I was on the rock. He brought me the white-tailed deer, and the rain, and you. And mebbe — mebbe there is something to this, and we need to get to know Him better."

Well, she was ready. It was time to put away the myths and superstitions for a God who had loved her from the beginning of time. And time to let God take care of Ireland.

"I'll talk to Caroline," she said. "You can talk to Michael. Maybe we'll all talk to each other. About God, I mean." She scooted closer, and Pace lifted her hand and kissed it. Warmth flowed through her that had nothing to do with the fire.

"It's a waste of time since you've already gone and said it." His brown eyes held hers, steady and sober, but with a new light from within. "But the man still likes to do the askin'. Oona Cathleen Moriarty, will you marry me and build a life with me in Oregon Country?"

"Faith, and I will." She had never been so certain of anything.

He kissed her, slow, deep, and satisfying, and she rested her head on his shoulder and watched the flames dance.

"Oona?"

"Yes?"

314

"I had a different name before. My Ma called me Paul Walker. Not sure I can go back to it bein' that it's from the past. But I got to ask you. Will you be marryin' Pace Williams or Paul Walker?"

Oona burrowed more deeply into his arms. "Both."

EPILOGUE

"Pace, my man. Isn't this the finest piece of horseflesh you ever saw?" Michael beamed down at the two-week-old foal.

Pace swallowed a mouthful of beans before answering. "Ain't bad."

"You'll be sayin' more than 'ain't bad' when you want the Missus to have her own mount. Or a pony for a little one."

Pace had to admit he was right. The foal, sired by Jenny's Rebel, looked to be a keeper. One more sign that Mike and Caroline — and Jenny — had made the right decision.

Mike wouldn't be a farmer, beyond digging a kitchen garden for Caroline. Mike and Jenny would be partners in this horse farm with Rebel as the first sire to a race of champions. They'd dug out a meadow from these forests, good grazing land. He ought to know, he'd helped them dig a future. He had the aching back to show for it. Mike and Caroline's rebuilt log home was on one edge of the property. Another log house sat at an another angle for the Jacksons, and Jenny's small cabin was on the other edge.

And today a community party honored their first foaling.

His gaze automatically sought out Oona, his wife of one year, and he found that she was doing the same. She sent him a fleeting smile from the serving table. Oona, who shared his nights in his own snug cabin. Who still worked at the store, but only 'til the babies started coming. Pace made enough money now, so whatever Oona earned went into a fund for bringing Tom and the others home to these mountains. Mike and Caroline were putting a little bit aside too. If they could locate the remaining Moriartys, it wouldn't be long before they were brought home to Oregon Country.

He looked down at the tin star on his shirt, which caught the spring sunlight and threw it back. He didn't like to wear it in social situations, but Oona had insisted. She was so proud of him, danged if he knew why. But this job as sheriff to a growing Hall's Mill used everything he'd ever learned, every skill he had, to help his new neighbors have better lives. He couldn't argue with that.

And he never could say no to Oona. Look at her now, tall and strong, her black braid swinging as she dished out beans and banter with the townspeople. A wisp of her laughter floated over to him and he smiled to himself. Oona made him laugh, kept his meals hot, and held him when the nightmares came, which happened less and less. *Thank You, Lord.*

Jenny moved easily between the men who talked horseflesh and the women serving food. Was there anything Jenny couldn't do? She'd made her dream happen too, here in the Klamath Mountains. She seemed happy. Never could tell with Jenny, probably never would, but the town respected her and she still had Rebel.

Caroline stood next to Oona, with her and Mike's baby on her hip, dishing out food with her free hand. Caroline was as gracious as ever, and she and Mike doted on their baby girl, a miniature Mike with black hair and big blue eyes. Maybe he and Oona could give her a cousin.

Mike hosted this gathering with his big voice and bigger laugh. He couldn't ask for a better friend. Mike was a leader in their community, a man who'd found his true home.

And what a community it was. Moses

Jackson, Mike and Jenny's foreman, hoisted a small white child on the back of an easygoing nag.

Elijah Jackson and Zeb Wilkins stuffed their faces with all the free food, while little Deborah Jackson played hopscotch with a group of girls.

Mrs. Jackson huddled at a makeshift table with ol' Mary Alice Wilkins, their heads bent over a fashion magazine from the East, Miz Wilkins' long finger pointing something out.

Molly shepherded her two adopted children, Sadie and young Lucas, making sure they had vegetables on their plates, probably throwing in a proverb for good measure.

A new teacher, a new doctor, and a circuit-riding preacher had all come to this place.

With grit and work and a little shed blood, they had made something new in these woods.

Here Oona came, bearing her own plate of food, her face shining and her hair gleaming in the spring sunlight. Her smile was only for him. He moved aside on the fallen log, and she tucked her skirts around her as she sat next to him.

"Caroline said I needed to take a break and get something to eat myself. She's like a little mother to me, Pace, sure and she is."

"Well, sure and I'm glad of the company," he retorted, his free hand finding hers under the folds of her skirt.

He would serve her, and serve these people, 'til his Lord called him home.

A DEVOTIONAL MOMENT

Do not take revenge, my dear friends, but
leave room for God's wrath, for it is
written: "It is mine to avenge; I will repay,"
says the Lord. ~ Romans 12:19

Most of us have a sense of justice; we
understand and often react with anger when
something is wrong or not fair, and sometimes we try to exact justice ourselves.
Christians are taught that justice will be
served by God when the time is right. One
of the most difficult things to do is to wait
for that justice. Whether it is for someone
else to come to their senses, or a person of
authority to take notice, or even the courts
to decide, the need for justice can be a long,
arduous road. Christians are encouraged to
rely on God for justice, even when the wait
is long. We even may not see justice done in
our lifetime, but God always serves us well,
and we can rest in the knowledge that

justice will come about, either in this life or the next.

In **Settlers' Hope,** the protagonist has given up on God. She is so outraged by injustice that she closes her mind to all possibilities of happiness. Revenge is in her heart, and she will not rest until those who wreaked havoc on her beloved family are brought to justice. But God isn't finished in her life yet.

Recall a time when you felt injustice acutely, whether it was something that happened to you directly, to someone you love, or in your community. Regardless of how you chose to act then, resolve now always to let God be the avenger. Remember that when injustice happens, rely on God. To seek revenge yourself does nothing but steal your faith and your peace — and your revenge is never as effective or eloquent as that which God doles out. Yes, fight injustice by always standing firm for what is right and just, but mark that line between doing what you can and then letting God do the rest and falling into a state of wrath and letting anger and vengeance consume you.

LORD, WHEN AN INJUSTICE HAPPENS IN

MY LIFE, PLEASE GIVE ME THE STRENGTH TO SAY, "THY WILL BE DONE." IN JESUS' NAME I PRAY, AMEN.

ABOUT THE AUTHOR

Kathleen Bailey is a journalist and novelist with 40 years' experience in the nonfiction, newspaper and inspirational fields. Born in 1951, she was a child in the 50s, a teen in the 60s, a young adult in the 70s and a young mom in the 80s. It's been a turbulent, colorful time to grow up, and she's enjoyed every minute of it and written about most of it.

Bailey's work includes both historical and contemporary fiction, with an underlying thread of men and women finding their way home, to Christ and each other.

The employees of Thorndike Press hope you have enjoyed this Large Print book. All our Thorndike, Wheeler, and Kennebec Large Print titles are designed for easy reading, and all our books are made to last. Other Thorndike Press Large Print books are available at your library, through selected bookstores, or directly from us.

For information about titles, please call:
  (800) 223-1244

or visit our website at:
  gale.com/thorndike

To share your comments, please write:
  Publisher
  Thorndike Press
  10 Water St., Suite 310
  Waterville, ME 04901